# BLACK RIVER

John Dyer has come to the insignificant little town of Black River to destroy the last living reminder of his dark past. He has come to kill. Jack Hart is determined to stop him. Only he knows the terrible truth that has driven Dyer here, and he knows that only he can beat Dyer in a gunfight. Ex-lawman Brad Harris is after Dyer too — to avenge his family. The stage is set for madness, death and vengeance.

ADAM WRIGHT

# BLACK RIVER

*Complete and Unabridged*

## LINFORD
### Leicester

First published in Great Britain in 1997 by
Robert Hale Limited
London

First Linford Edition
published 1999
by arrangement with
Robert Hale Limited
London

British Library CIP Data

Wright, A. (Adam)
    Black River.—Large print ed.—
Linford western library
1. Western stories
2. Large type books
I. Title
823.9'14 [F]

ISBN 0–7089–5477–4

Published by
F. A. Thorpe (Publishing) Ltd.
Anstey, Leicestershire
Set by Words & Graphics Ltd.
Anstey, Leicestershire
Printed and bound in Great Britain by
T. J. International Ltd., Padstow, Cornwall

This book is printed on acid-free paper

For two good friends;
Gill and Rashpal.
With thanks and appreciation

# 1

The seven riders came thundering out of the dawn, their mounts' hooves spraying an angry cloud of dust in their wake. As they approached his ranch house, Andy Carlson guessed that they were trying to outrun the storm which loomed dark and threatening over the mountains behind them. Winter had begun to seize Idaho in its icy grip and those dark clouds would surely break soon and shed their load of snow. The riders would need shelter until the worst of it had passed.

Andy headed toward the house to tell his son, Todd, to get coffee brewing. He wished his wife and eldest son hadn't gone to town. Liz made better coffee than Todd.

As he reached the porch, though, and took a second look at the seven riders, his stomach knotted tightly. He couldn't put a finger on it but there was something about those seven dark shapes silhouetted against the stormy mountains and dull dawn light which sent a chill of panic through him. It was something indefinable, yet when Andy entered the kitchen, he felt scared enough to grab his gunbelt from the wall where it hung and fasten it around his waist. He watched the seven men through the kitchen window as they rode on to his property and headed toward the house.

'Pa, do you think it's gonna snow?' Todd had come into the kitchen. He looked up at Andy and, seeing some of the panic in his father's eyes, followed his gaze out the kitchen window. 'We got visitors,' he said.

'Todd,' Andy said. 'I want you to go up to your room until I call you.'

The boy regarded his father closely. 'Do you think those fellers are outlaws?' he asked excitedly. At ten, Todd thought being an outlaw was a glamorous way of life.

'I don't know,' Andy replied seriously. 'Now you go on up to your room while I talk to them and find out who they are.' The seven men outside had dismounted and were casting glances around the corrals and stables. Andy fumbled the Smith & Wesson revolver from his holster and checked the weapon was fully loaded before heading out to the porch.

He nodded to the seven strangers and they watched him as he stepped off the porch. Their faces were expressionless but they seemed to exude an aura of animosity. 'Howdy,' Andy said, trying to hide the nervousness in his voice. His fear was unfounded, he knew, but up close these seven men with their forbidding countenances scared him. Hell, they looked like trouble.

Big trouble.

The tallest, a wiry man with a black beard stepped forward and held out his hand. Andy shook it. 'Howdy yourself,' the tall man said. 'Name's John Dyer and these are my friends.' He squeezed

3

Andy's hand hard and when he released it, Andy's knuckles were sore.

'Andy Carlson,' Andy said. 'I guess you'll be wanting shelter from the storm.'

Dyer glanced at the dark clouds sweeping over the mountains, considered a moment, then said, 'Nah. We should be able to outrun it.'

Andy tried to hide his relief at the news. To outrun those clouds, the men would have to leave soon. Perhaps they would just water their horses and go.

'We been outrunning a lot of things lately,' Dyer continued. 'Ain't that right, boys?'

The other men laughed harshly.

Dyer chuckled. 'You see, Mr Carlson, that's why we headed for your place as soon as we saw it. Back there,' he flicked a thumb at the mountains, 'is a feller who's been following us. Now we don't know who he is or why he'd want to follow honest men like ourselves.'

The others laughed again.

'But the fact is that he's been on our

trail for the past two days and that just makes us nervous. So while me and my friends outrun that storm, Joe here is gonna wait in your house until this feller turns up. Then Joe is gonna find out who he is and teach him that we don't like people on our tails.'

Andy tried to look calmly at Dyer. 'I don't want any trouble, mister.'

Dyer returned Andy's stare and in that look, Andy saw a darkness which tightened the knot of fear in his stomach. It wasn't just the dark eyes and mean stare; it was something *behind* the stare. Andy felt as if he had just glimpsed John Dyer's dark, twisted soul.

'Well you got trouble, Mister Carlson,' Dyer said evenly. 'My name doesn't mean anything to you, does it?'

Andy shook his head.

'Well a hell of a lot of folk east of those mountains know who I am. I've killed nine men, Mr Carlson. Don't make it ten. Joe, get yourself settled in the house and wait for our friend to arrive. We'll ride on to Bull's Creek and meet you there.'

A short, stocky man with a Winchester headed for the porch.

'No,' Andy said. He didn't want them in his house. Todd was in there.

But Todd had come out on to the porch. He looked at Dyer's men and at his father's panicked face. 'Pa,' he said, 'what's goin' on?'

Dyer looked at the boy for a moment then approached him. 'Howdy, son,' he said, affecting a friendly manner.

Andy's panic became blind. He couldn't have Dyer near his son. Before he knew what he was doing, he had pulled the Smith & Wesson and levelled it at Dyer's head. 'Stop right there, Mr Dyer,' he said. The calmness in his own voice surprised him.

Dyer stopped and turned to face Andy. He looked at the Smith & Wesson and chuckled. 'Mr Carlson, you don't want to shoot me. I was just going to say hello to your fine boy.'

'Get away from him,' Andy said,

6

gesturing with the gun. He kept an eye on the other six men in case any of them went for a weapon.

Dyer stood square on to Andy. 'Mr Carlson,' he said flatly, 'are you afraid to die?'

The question took Andy by surprise and while he was considering it, Dyer's hand became a blur. Andy caught the flash of movement and squeezed the trigger of his gun. As he did so, he realized that he had never killed a man before. Dyer would be his first.

But Andy's bullet went wide, embedding itself in the wood of the porch, because by the time he had let off the shot, Dyer's own gun had barked loudly and a slug had sent Andy reeling to the dirt. Before he understood what had happened, he was on the ground and it hurt to breathe.

'Pa!' Todd came running over to him, and knelt beside him, tears streaming down his cheeks.

Dyer walked over and looked down at Andy. 'Ten's a more round number, anyway,' he said. He holstered his gun and walked away laughing.

Andy could feel his life ebbing away. A numbness spread over him. He looked up at his son. 'Todd, when you get a chance, run. Take one of the horses. Head for town and find Ethan and your mother.' He lifted a hand to the boy's cheek and wiped away a tear. The hand became heavy and Andy let it drop to the ground. He lay there looking at the sky a moment. 'Storm's coming,' he said weakly. Then he closed his eyes and died.

★ ★ ★

By the time the first flakes of snow tumbled to the ground, Dyer and his men had watered their horses and were ready to move off. Joe stood on the porch with his Winchester, his horse stabled behind the house.

Todd shivered as he knelt over his father's body. A cold wind had accompanied the storm from the mountains and it blew angrily around the ranch.

Dyer stood watching the mountains. 'He'll be coming soon, Joe,' he said to the man on the porch. 'Probably just some pissante sheriff. He can't be too smart coming after all seven of us on his own. You shouldn't have any trouble handling him.'

Joe nodded. 'What do you want me to do with the kid?'

Dyer looked at Todd and stroked his beard. 'Make sure he doesn't warn that feller on our backtrail. Keep him locked up inside.'

'And then?' Joe asked.

Dyer shrugged. 'Whatever you feel comfortable with, Joe. It doesn't really matter. We'll meet you at Bull's Creek.' He swung on to his horse and spurred it forward. The other five followed and soon they vanished into the snowy distance.

'Hey, kid,' Joe said from the porch. 'You'd better get inside.' He gestured to the house with his rifle.

Todd remained next to his father. He was determined not to do anything this man told him to do. His opinion on outlaws had changed drastically since the shooting of his father.

'I said get inside,' Joe said angrily. 'When that storm hits, you don't want to be out of doors.'

'Doesn't matter,' Todd said. 'You're gonna kill me anyways. Just like you killed my pa.'

Joe came over to him and knelt to face him. Todd expected the outlaw to grab him and drag him inside but instead Joe said, 'I didn't kill your pa, kid. And I ain't gonna kill you. You heard what John said. It doesn't matter what I do with ya. So I could just leave you locked up when I ride out. Someone'll find ya.'

'You're an outlaw,' Todd said. 'You could be lying to me and I wouldn't even know it.'

'Look, I ain't gonna kill no kid.'

Todd looked at him. 'My pa was a good man,' he said softly. 'He never

10

hurt no one.' He began to cry again.

'Come on inside,' Joe said. He took Todd's arm and guided him indoors.

In the kitchen, Joe glanced out of the window toward the mountains. 'Damn, I can't see anything with all this snow,' he growled. 'Come on, kid, I'm gonna lock ya in the bedroom for a spell.'

He led Todd upstairs to the master bedroom. Todd sat on his ma and pa's bed while Joe heaved a wardrobe in front of the window. 'I don't reckon you'll be able to move that,' he said. 'Now you stay put.' He left the room and Todd heard the key rattle in the lock, trapping him. He heard the stairs creak as Joe went back downstairs.

Todd sat on the bed, crying softly for his pa for a while, then wiped his tears away with the sleeve of his shirt. He thought about his ma and Ethan. If Ethan were here, he'd know what to do. Ethan was strong and decisive and a lot older than Todd. Todd had always thought he would be just like Ethan but now, for the first time in his life, he realized that he was just a kid. And he was scared. Joe might have been telling the truth about not killing him but Joe was an outlaw and outlaws couldn't be trusted.

He got up off the bed and looked at the heavy wardrobe blocking the window. Putting his back to it, he strained every muscle in his body to push it out of the way. He gritted his teeth and sweated. The wardrobe's wooden panels dug painfully into his shoulder blades.

It didn't budge.

He sat on the bed again and considered his position. In desperation, he walked over to the door and tried the handle in case Joe had not locked it properly. He had.

There was no way out except the window, and the wardrobe blocked the window. And he couldn't move the wardrobe. He sat on the bed and sighed, resting his head in his hands. He stared at the wardrobe, the only thing blocking his way to freedom.

He got an idea.

He pulled the wardrobe door open and pulled out the clothes hanging inside, scattering them over the floor. When he had emptied the wardrobe, he looked at the back panel. Now, only that single piece of wood blocked the way to the window. Todd gripped both edges of the wardrobe and lashed out at the back of the wardrobe with his foot. The resulting *crack* of his boot on the wood made him cringe. What if Joe heard the noise from downstairs?

Todd crept across the room and listened at the bedroom door for a moment. Silence.

He returned to the wardrobe and inspected the back panel. A slim crack ran down the length of the wood. Todd kicked at it again and the crack widened, letting daylight from the window beyond seep into the wardrobe. He kicked again and the back panel split and fell to the floor with a *crackle* of splintering timber. Beyond lay the window.

Todd wiped the sweat from his brow and crossed to the bedroom door again. The panel had made a lot of noise when it had broken and he wanted to be sure Joe hadn't heard anything from below. Todd listened for a tell-tale creaking on the stairs but heard nothing.

He ran to the window and unlatched it. Gripping the frame, he lifted, expecting the window to give easily. Instead, it creaked open an inch and stuck. The cold outside had warped the wood. Todd put his hands through the opening and gripped the window from below. A bitter wind howled around the house, whipping the snow into swirling shapes. It chilled Todd's fingers and blew chill air into the room through the small gap in the window.

He strained his shoulders and back and pulled up against the wood. The frame squealed loudly and the window moved up then stuck again. Todd didn't have the strength to pull it open further.

But the gap was wide enough for him to squeeze through. Shivering with cold, he angled his body through the half-open window. It was just a short drop to the snow-covered porch roof below. Todd threw a leg over the sill.

And heard the bedroom door crash open behind him. Joe rushed into the room and shouted, 'Goddammit, get back here!'

Todd quickly swung his other leg over the sill and let gravity pull his body down. He held on to the window-frame with his fingers, ready to drop to the porch roof.

Joe leapt across the room and grabbed Todd's arms with both hands. 'You ain't going nowhere, kid,' he said angrily. 'That feller is nearly here. I can't risk you warnin' him.'

'Let go of me,' Todd squealed. He swung his body in an effort to make Joe let go but the outlaw's grip was strong.

'I mean it,' Joe said. He let go of Todd's left arm and pulled a six-gun from his holster. He pointed it out the window, at Todd's face. 'Now get back in here!'

Todd lunged forward and bit Joe's left hand hard. The outlaw roared in pain and released his grip. Todd fell to the porch roof. He twisted his body as he fell in an attempt to land on his feet. He managed to plant his boots on the roof but the snow was wet and slippery. Todd's feet shot out from under him and he slid toward the edge of the roof. He rolled on to his stomach and tried to grip something to stop his fall but all he grabbed were handfuls of wet snow. He felt his legs go over the edge of the roof and the rest of his body followed.

He landed in the yard painfully and gasped as the air shot out of his lungs. Winded, he rolled on to his stomach and managed to push himself to his knees. He knelt there, sucking cold air into his body and wiping the tears from his eyes. In the distance, through the swirling snow, he could see a rider mounted on a black stallion approaching the ranch slowly and warily.

He knew he could escape now. The stables were only a few yards away and he could easily get a horse and ride into town. But if he did that, he couldn't warn the feller riding toward him about Joe. The outlaw was probably lurking in the kitchen with his Winchester. Todd hesitated, unsure of his next move.

He knew what Ethan would do if he were here and that decided him. He got to his feet and ran across the snow to the stranger, shouting, 'Look out, mister! He's in the house!'

The wind whipped his words away but the rider must have heard him because he dropped from the stallion and pulled a rifle from the saddleboot. The movement was swift and fluid.

Glass crashed behind Todd and he realized Joe had smashed the kitchen window with the barrel of the Winchester. He sprawled headlong into the snow and crawled toward the corral fence. It offered scant cover but it was all that was available.

A shot rang out from the house.

The black stallion bolted at the sound. The stranger dropped to one knee and for a moment, Todd thought he had been hit, but then realized he was just steadying himself. He aimed his rifle at the kitchen window and fired. The glass shattered.

The stranger jumped to his feet and ran toward Todd. Although he was wrapped in a scarf, gloves and long coat, he ran swiftly across the yard, holding his black hat to his head with one hand while the arm holding the rifle pumped strongly to lend him momentum.

Joe fired from the kitchen window again but the shot went wild.

The stranger levered another round into the chamber of his weapon and fired one-handed at the house, covering his run across the open space of the yard. He shouted something at Todd

18

but the wind obscured his words. He shouted again as he got closer. 'Get into the barn!'

The barn was on the other side of the corral. To get there, Todd would have to run through the horses which were already nervous with all the gunfire. But if he stayed here, he would surely be hit eventually. He climbed over the fence and sprinted across the corral.

The horses panicked and bolted around the enclosure. Todd closed his eyes and ran as fast as he could, praying that he would avoid the animals' hooves. He heard shots from the house again but ignored them. The horses were all around him, running in blind panic, their bodies pressing close to him, threatening to knock him over and trample him. Somehow, he made it to the far fence unhurt.

He climbed through the railings and ran into the barn. Exhausted and cold, he dropped to the sweet-smelling hay and lay there, catching his breath. Beyond the barn door, he saw the stranger vault over the corral fence as a bullet thumped into wood near him. He returned fire and raced across the corral, leaping over the fence nearest the barn. His hat blew off and Todd noticed the man was black. He hadn't seen many black men before but he had certainly never seen a black lawman so he wondered if this was actually the feller who had been trailing Dyer and his men.

The black stranger entered the barn. He gripped his rifle in both hands and cast a cautious glance around the barn door toward the house.

Todd walked over to him. 'Are you a lawman, mister?'

'Stay back, son,' the stranger said, waving an arm toward the back of the barn. 'I don't want you to get hurt.'

Todd returned to the hay and sat down again.

'No, I'm not a lawman,' the stranger said as he watched the house. The shooting had stopped and the only noise was the soft moan of the wind and the patter of snow against the barn roof. 'Name's Jack Hart,' the black man said. He turned from the door and knelt down to face Todd, holding out his gloved hand.

Todd shook it and started at the strange feel of the man's grip. When they released the handshake, he realized that Jack had lost the little and ring fingers of his right hand. Those two fingers of his glove had been removed and the leather sewn shut.

'My name's Todd Carlson,' he said.

'Nice to meet you, Todd,' Jack said. He returned to the barn door and glanced at the house.

'They killed my pa,' Todd said. He didn't know why he said that but he felt that he had to tell someone. Maybe he wouldn't believe it himself until he actually said the words.

Jack looked at him. His dark eyes seemed soft and kind. 'I'm sorry,' he said. 'I truly am sorry.'

Todd nodded and held back the tears that threatened to burst from him. 'If you're not a lawman,' he said, 'are you a bounty hunter?'

Jack shook his head. 'How many of them are in the house, Todd?'

'Just one. His name's Joe.'

Jack nodded slightly. 'Joe Bragg,' he said softly.

'Do you know him?' Todd asked.

Jack risked a glance around the barn door. A shot sounded from the house and Jack ducked his head back as wood splintered from the barn wall. 'I don't know him,' he told Todd. 'But I know of him. He's not the one I'm after but he rides with him.'

'Who are you after?' Todd asked.

'Dyer.' Jack almost spat the name out, as if saying it left a disgusting taste in his mouth.

'He's the feller who shot my pa,' Todd said quietly. He thought of his father lying dead in the yard and he began to cry softly. He wanted his ma to return from town with Ethan. He needed to feel her arms around him.

'Listen,' Jack said, still peeking at

the house. 'We can't stay here all morning. We'll freeze to death.' He looked at Todd shivering on the hay and removed his long black coat. He laid it gently over Todd's shoulders. The warmth of the fleece-lined garment stopped the boy's shivering.

Jack moved to the door. He was dressed in a darkblue shirt and black pants. He wore a gun rig with the holster on the left side. He also wore a black waistcoat and as he turned, something on that waistcoat flashed in the morning light. A silver star.

Todd gasped. 'You said you weren't a lawman.'

'I'm not,' Jack said. 'At least, not by profession.'

'But you're wearing a sheriff's star.'

Jack shook his head. 'Not sheriff's; deputy US marshal.' He pumped a shell into the chamber of his rifle. 'I'm gonna have to get to the house,' he said. 'You stay put and out of the way until I come back to fetch you.'

Todd nodded. 'OK.'

Jack put a hand on the boy's shoulder, grinned reassuringly, turned to the door and stepped out into the storm.

* * *

As soon as he stepped into the howling wind and whipping snow, Jack sprinted for the porch of the house. He fired his Winchester in the direction of the kitchen window to cover himself and reached the porch without drawing fire from the house. He stood on the porch by the front door, shivering as the wind cut through his shirt like a shard of ice.

He leant his Winchester against the house and drew his Peacemaker with his left hand. He hadn't been born left-handed but since his fingers had been shot off, he had been forced to relearn everything with his good left hand. It had been a slow, painful process but Jack had learned patiently. Whenever he had faltered or thought

24

of giving up, he had motivated himself by remembering his brother. On the few occasions when that failed, he had thought about what he was going to do to Dyer when he caught up with him. Jack had learned well.

Thumbing back the Colt's hammer, he gently turned the handle of the door and entered the house.

In the hallway, he paused and listened, gun ready in case Joe Bragg was hiding somewhere, ready to jump him. The house remained silent. The only sound came from the wind whistling through the eaves. Jack crept along the hallway toward the rear of the house.

The kitchen was empty. Spent shell casings littered the floor, gradually being covered over by the snow which blew through the jagged remains of the window. Jack's boots crunched over the broken glass shards and he whirled towards the door in case the sound had brought Bragg. But the house remained quiet.

The sound of horses whinnying outside made Jack curse. Bragg was in the stable behind the house. He was making a run for it!

Jack ran along the hallway and reached the porch in time to see Bragg riding hell for leather out of the stable. Jack holstered the Peacemaker and picked up the Winchester. With his left hand on the trigger and his right steadying the barrel, he sighted on the fleeing figure and fired. The sound of the shot reverberated around the porch.

Bragg fell from his horse and hit the ground heavily. A cloud of disturbed snow puffed up around him then settled again over his dead body. The horse continued to run.

Jack watched the unmoving body for a moment then turned and walked back through the storm to fetch the boy from the barn.

# 2

Liz Carlson sat crying in the sitting room, holding Todd tightly to her chest. He was crying with her. Jack stood quietly across the room, watching them sadly. This is why I have to stop Dyer, he reminded himself. So he can't cause any more pain for any more people. He thought of his brother for a moment before pushing the thoughts away. He had things to do.

It was past noon. Liz and Ethan had returned from town an hour ago and both had taken the news of Andy's death badly. Liz had broken down and held on to Todd as if she were afraid she might lose him if she let go.

Ethan, on the other hand, had not cried, had not even struggled to hold back tears. Instead, he had busied himself with the digging of a grave for his father. He was outside now, in the snow, digging before the ground froze. To all outward appearances, Ethan seemed unmoved by the death of his father. But Jack knew the boy was taking the news hard. He could see a flicker of vengeance burning in the seventeen-year-old's eyes. And that, Jack knew, was dangerous. Better to cry and expel the grief now than keep it bottled up waiting to explode violently later.

He decided to go out and talk to the boy. Grabbing his coat and shrugging it on, he left the house and walked out back where Ethan was bent over the ground, attacking it with a shovel. The wind had dropped to a cold breeze which sent waves of powdered snow whispering over the ranch.

Jack approached the boy and nodded. Ethan stopped his digging and leant on the shovel handle. He looked closely at Jack. 'I guess I should thank you for saving Todd's life,' he said.

'I just wish I'd gotten here sooner,' Jack replied.

Ethan gazed at the ground, lost in his own thoughts for a moment before saying, 'You think you can catch those men?'

Jack nodded. 'I'll try my best.'

'Because it's your job?' Ethan nodded at the star, visible beneath Jack's open coat.

Jack gazed at the mountains in the distance, watching the dark winter clouds spread over the rocky peaks. 'It's not my job,' he told Ethan. 'I became a marshal for one reason and one reason only: I want Dyer. This star just makes it legal.'

'I want him too,' Ethan said flatly.

Jack nodded. 'Of course you do, he killed your pa.'

'I want to come with you.'

Jack shook his head. 'I can't allow that.'

Anger flared up suddenly in Ethan's eyes. His lips pressed together tightly. 'Why not?'

Jack put a hand on the boy's shoulder. 'Two reasons, Ethan. You're needed here. You have to take care of your ma and Todd now. It's up to you to run the ranch. You can't turn your back on that kind of responsibility to get involved in a manhunt.'

Ethan seemed to consider this. He looked around at the ranch; his responsibility now. The anger within him seemed to burn out. He nodded slowly. 'I guess you're right, Mr Hart. But what's the second reason?'

'You can't beat him,' Jack said. 'If it came down to a gunfight, you wouldn't have a chance.'

'Is he that good?'

Jack nodded. 'He's quicker than you could imagine, Ethan.'

'And you think you can beat him?' Ethan asked.

Jack watched a distant storm roll over the mountains. 'Yeah,' he said. 'If it comes down to it, I can beat him.'

'How can you know that?'

'I know,' Jack said. A memory came to him but he dispelled it.

Perhaps Ethan had noticed something

cross Jack's face because he seemed to decide not to press the subject any further. Instead, he said, 'Mr Hart, I feel like no matter what happens to those men, it won't take away what I'm feeling inside.'

Jack nodded slowly. 'Maybe it won't, son. Maybe it won't.' He knew the boy was finally coming to terms with his feelings about his father's death. He decided to leave him to it. He turned and walked through the winter wind toward the house.

'Mr Hart?' Ethan called from behind him.

Jack turned to face the boy.

'Is your pa still alive?'

Taken aback by the question, Jack nodded. 'Yeah,' he said. 'He's getting on in years but he's still alive. Lives in Colorado.'

Ethan looked at the snow shifting over the ground. 'So you don't really know how I feel.'

Jack thought of his brother. 'I know, Ethan,' he said. 'I know.'

The boy nodded and returned to digging his father's grave. Jack saw his shoulders hitch a couple of times. He was either crying or trying to hold back the tears. They would come eventually, Jack knew.

When he got back to the house, Liz Carlson was in the kitchen fixing dinner. The room was chilled by the wind creeping around the board Jack had fixed over the shattered window while he and Todd waited for Liz and Ethan to return from town. She scurried around the kitchen, trying to absorb herself in the cooking and trying to forget, just for a moment, the tragedy that had befallen her family. Jack watched her and sat at the kitchen table.

'Mr Hart,' she said as she continued to busy herself with the stove, 'I'd appreciate it if you would join us for dinner. If you'd like to stay overnight, I could . . . '

'Dinner would be fine, ma'am,' Jack said. 'After that, I'd best be on my way.

I've got some things to attend to.'

'Of course,' she said. She turned from the stove to face him. She was pretty and Jack could imagine that under different circumstances, she might even be beautiful. But, at the moment, her beauty had been trampled by grief. Her eyes were dark-rimmed and red, she looked pale and drawn.

'You won't stop until you've caught him, will you,' she said evenly. It seemed more statement than question.

'No, ma'am, I won't,' Jack replied.

'No,' she said. 'Because he's hurt you too in some way, hasn't he?'

Jack's gaze involuntarily strayed to his damaged right hand. 'He's hurt a lot of people, ma'am.'

She looked at his hand, nodded, and returned to the cooking.

★ ★ ★

The dark shade of evening crept over the ranch as Jack prepared to leave. The wind had died now and the snowfall had been reduced to a few fluttering flakes. The temperature had plummeted to well below freezing and Jack had fixed a blanket over his stallion, beneath the saddle, to keep the horse warm during the night ride ahead.

Liz, Ethan and Todd stood on the porch watching him as he swung himself over the saddle. 'Ethan,' Jack said. 'If you take Joe Bragg's body to the law office in town, there'll be a reward.'

Ethan shook his head. 'That belongs to you, Mr Hart.'

'No,' Jack said. 'I know it's no compensation for what happened to your pa but the money'll come in handy. Besides, I don't have time to worry about it. I want to get to Bull's Creek before Dyer moves on.'

Liz stepped forward. 'We're all obliged to you, Mr Hart.'

Jack touched the brim of his hat.

'We wish you luck,' she said.

'Take care of yourselves,' Jack said.

He urged the horse into a trot and rode away from the ranch.

He only looked back once and when he did, they were still standing by the house, watching him leave. They waved and he waved back. This morning, he thought, they were probably happy. A family. Probably thought they had all the time in the world together. All that has been destroyed in one day by one man.

Dyer.

His thoughts turned to the fragility of his own family and the black storm that had swept through it and destroyed it. He urged the stallion on into the hills as dark night fell over the land.

*So fragile*.

# 3

Brad Harris, sheriff of Bull's Creek, had been plagued by one simple question for the past week. And now, at Frank Simpson's funeral, he asked himself again: *Do I belong here?*

He watched the mourners gathered around the old man's grave. He knew them all, had lived amongst them for the past seven years. For five of those years, he had been their sheriff. But still he felt like an outsider.

Bracing himself against the cold wind, he turned from the graveside and walked across the small town cemetery. Maybe one day he would be buried here, dead of old age like Frank. Or maybe he would be gunned down on the street. After all, being a sheriff could be dangerous. But not in Bull's Creek. The town was a small, sleepy affair and the most risk Brad had undertaken while keeping law here was to put drunks in his cells overnight to keep them from disturbing the peace. He had an easy job.

Maybe that was the problem. Perhaps he missed the excitement he had been used to during his early years.

He had fought in the war. He had only been eighteen when he had enlisted to fight the rebels. And he had seen action. When that conflict was over, Brad had drifted for a while before working ranches in Montana. He had learned a lot about horses and cattle. When he had tired of that and drifted on again, he had ended up here, in Bull's Creek. He didn't know why he had decided to stay here. He just had. And he had become sheriff.

Now he was tired of that and ready to move on again.

He looked back at the mourners. Dressed in black, they stood out against the snowy mountain landscape like dark shadows. They had all come to this town at some time and stayed, same as Brad. But unlike Brad, they had become content here. He envied them.

When he reached the main street, he headed along the boardwalk in the direction of his office. He was cold and needed a mug of hot coffee inside him. He also needed to consider his plans for the future.

Inside his office, he stoked up the stove and removed his coat and hat.

Settling behind his desk, he lit a smoke and fixed coffee. Beyond the frost-rimed window, the folk of Bull's Creek went about their daily business. Brad watched them and drank his coffee. These people had built lives here, raised their children here. Brad had not even found a wife.

It was not through lack of opportunity; the town had its share of unmarried pretty women and, because he was sheriff and good-looking himself, more than a few had shown an interest in becoming Mrs Harris. But, somehow, Brad had stopped himself becoming serious with any of them. He had always felt that his future lay elsewhere.

He went over to the window and gazed at the mountains. Beyond those snow-covered peaks stretched a world he had almost forgotten. Living in Bull's Creek for so long had isolated him. This town had enveloped him in its secure grip and had *become* the world for him. Now he was remembering that there was more.

Finding the picture had reminded him.

He settled into his chair again and rummaged through his desk drawer, leafing through the sheaf of Wanted posters until he found the old, creased photograph. He laid it on the desktop and stared at it, drawing deeply on his smoke.

He was in that photograph, along with his parents and his sister, Laura. They stood in front of their ranch house in Wyoming, smiling proudly at the camera, their futures stretching out before them.

Brad looked at the smile on his face in the picture. He had been fifteen. Three years later, he had left to fight in the war. He hadn't seen his family since.

*Why didn't I go back after the war?*

He knew the answer to that. His father. They had never got on together.

Brad's father had been a strict disciplinarian, pushing his son all the time. Brad, being young, had taken this to mean that he could never be good enough for his pa. Whatever he did, however hard he tried, his father never praised him, just pushed him to try even harder next time. So, after the war, Brad had seized the opportunity to get away from his pa for good and had drifted west. The photograph on his desk was the only link he had with his family.

And the Raven, he reminded himself.

He reached under his shirt and pulled on the slim chain around his neck. The Raven talisman hung from his fingers, glinting silvery in the sunlight coming through the windows. Brad's mother and sister had given it to him before he had left to go to war. It was an Indian amulet, shaped like the Raven which the Indians believed had created the world. Laura and his mother had given it to Brad to bring him luck and protect him from the rebels.

Brad wondered if his next move should be to visit his family. He didn't know if they still lived in Wyoming, though. He didn't even know if they were all still alive.

He pushed the Raven back under his shirt and blew a cloud of smoke toward the ceiling, watching its grey-white tendrils curl and scatter in the air. He stubbed out the glowing butt in the ashtray on his desk. Swallowing the last of the hot coffee, he shrugged on his coat, placed his hat on his head and went out into the street.

He had a big decision to make and for Brad, that meant riding his pinto into the mountains. He always thought clearer when he was away from the town and in the saddle.

He got to Josh Gibson's livery barn and started to put the tack on his horse. Josh let him keep his saddle in the barn for free because he was the sheriff. The ostler watched Brad from the stall opposite where he was lovingly grooming a big bay. Josh loved horses.

'It ain't good weather for riding,' the ostler offered, as Brad tightened the saddle cinch. 'Snow will have cut off most of the trails.'

'I'm not going far, Josh,' Brad said. 'Just got to clear my head.'

Josh nodded as if he knew what Brad meant. 'Mind you,' he said. 'One of the eastern trails must still be passable. Six fellers rode in last night. Said they came from the east.'

Brad slipped his Henry rifle into the saddleboot. He wasn't expecting trouble but in this country, a man didn't go riding without a firearm. Before leading the horse out of the stall, he also checked his Colt Navy revolver. 'These fellers say why they were in town?' he asked Josh. Strangers were rare in Bull's Creek.

Josh shook his head. 'Just passing through, I guess.'

Brad nodded, led his horse outside and swung himself up. He hadn't been riding for a long time. It felt good to be in the saddle again. He set off east out of town toward the snowy mountains. He sniffed the fresh, crisp air and smiled to himself. At this moment, riding his horse along the eastern trail in the fresh-smelling, rugged country, he felt revitalized and alive.

He couldn't know that a rider was heading toward town on that trail; someone who would change everything for Brad. And he couldn't know that today would be his last in Bull's Creek and that soon he would be in the saddle for a very long time.

★ ★ ★

Jack had been in the saddle all night and he felt tired. The cold wind which had relentlessly buffeted him seemed to have drained his strength. There were times during the night, while following the snowy trail in the dark, that he had almost turned back for the Carlson house to wait until morning. But whenever doubt had forced itself into his mind, he had forced it out again with one thought: I'm closer now than I have ever been; he's within reach. He had kept going.

The few stops he had made were mainly to rest the stallion for a while. The horse was strong and Jack wanted to keep it that way. When he finally caught up with Dyer, he wanted to be ready for anything. Besides, the horse had been his constant companion for a long time and Jack felt an affection for the animal.

He had been riding along a trail through the pine and fir trees when he saw the rider coming toward him.

Gigging the stallion off the trail and into the trees, Jack slid from the saddle and drew his Winchester from the saddleboot. He tied the horse to a branch and found cover behind a group of young pine. He squinted to catch the rider's face. He knew Dyer's men by sight. It was possible that the outlaw had waited in Bull's Creek until it was obvious Joe Bragg was not going to arrive and then sent a man back along the trail to find out if they were still being followed. Jack levered a cartridge into the Winchester.

The rider didn't look as if he was searching for anyone. In fact, the tall man in the saddle seemed to be ambling along the trail aimlessly, wrapped up in his own thoughts. As he rode closer, Jack could make out his facial features. The face, with its steel-grey eyes, straight nose and high cheekbones, didn't belong to any of Dyer's men. Jack relaxed but kept a tight grip on the Winchester. Since he had started trailing Dyer, he was constantly on his guard, expecting trouble from any quarter. Only that way could he be ready to face it when it came. He stayed hidden in the trees.

The rider stopped his horse some distance along the trail and seemed to straighten almost imperceptibly in the saddle. He looked over his shoulder then into the trees on both sides of him as if he had sensed Jack's presence.

Jack felt his muscles tighten. He remained stock still, breathing shallowly as if the rider might hear his breathing and be alerted to his position.

The rider sat motionless in the saddle, his grey eyes scanning the trees. He slowly reached beneath his coat and pulled a Colt Navy revolver from his holster. He continued to watch the trees around him as he cocked it.

Jack felt sweat beading on his forehead. Maybe he was wrong about this man; maybe Dyer had hired him to come looking for Jack.

In the silence of the woods, the *click* of the Colt's hammer being cocked sounded loud and deadly.

Jack decided to risk revealing his presence. Otherwise, he might get into a gunfight with this man purely because they were on the same trail. 'Mister, I ain't looking for trouble,' he shouted. His voice broke the stillness of the snowy woods and somewhere a bird cried out raucously. Jack looked at his horse. The animal waited patiently among the trees. When Jack looked back at the trail, the stranger and *his* horse were gone.

★ ★ ★

Brad guided his pinto through the trees, his heart hammering in his chest and adrenalin coursing through him. He had sensed he was not alone in the woods when he had stopped. The shout coming from the trees had alarmed him and he had panicked, riding his horse off the trail and into the tight stand of pine to his right. He watched the trees and held the Colt ready.

'I said I don't want any trouble,' the deep voice shouted again. Brad strained to pick up the direction of the sound but the wind and trees made him unsure. He stopped his horse, dismounted, and crept forward through the knee-deep snow. He tethered the pinto to a fallen tree and shouted, 'Who is that calling?' He readied himself to gauge the direction of the voice.

'Who's asking?' came the reply. The shout seemed to come from behind a stand of pine directly ahead of him.

Brad took cover behind a large Douglas fir and watched those trees.

'Sheriff Brad Harris,' he called. 'Sheriff of Bull's Creek.'

'Sheriff?'

'Yeah,' Brad shouted. 'So come on out and show yourself.' He didn't like this situation. His nerves were on edge. 'This is the last time I complain about wanting some excitement,' he whispered to himself.

A sudden movement to his left surprised him and he spun around with the Colt at hip level. A black horse bolted along the trail, spraying snow in its wake. At first Brad thought

48

the stranger was making a run for it but then he realized the horse was riderless. He frowned, confused. Why would the stranger send his horse along the trail?

To divert my attention!

He spun back around and found himself staring into the barrel of a Winchester rifle. The black man holding the weapon smiled grimly. 'Drop the Colt,' he said evenly.

Brad felt his stomach knot. He had no choice but to obey the man's command. He uncocked his revolver and tossed it into the snow.

'Now,' the black man said. 'Tell me the truth. Did Dyer send you?'

'Dyer?' Brad shook his head. 'I've never heard of anyone called Dyer. I was just taking my morning ride out of town.'

'You say you're the sheriff of Bull's Creek?'

'That's what I told you,' Brad said. He opened his coat to reveal the star pinned to his shirt. He pointed to it. 'Sheriff,' he said.

The black man seemed to relax. He let the Winchester drop slightly and opened his own coat. 'Deputy US marshal,' he said, pointing to the star on his waistcoat. He held the rifle at his side and held out his right hand. 'Jack Hart,' he said amiably, all trace of his earlier hostility gone.

Brad looked at the hand and noticed the missing fingers. He shook it. 'Brad Harris,' he said. 'I don't mean any disrespect but I've never seen a black marshal before.'

Jack retrieved Brad's Colt from the ground, knocked the snow off it, and passed it to Brad. 'Well, to tell the truth,' he said, 'I've only been a marshal for a couple of weeks. I was sworn in at Denver so that when I catch the man I'm after, it'll be legal.'

'Would that be this Dyer fellow you mentioned?'

Jack nodded. 'Unless he's moved on already, he's in your town.'

Brad thought for a moment. 'Is he with five others?'

'Yeah, have you seen him? Is he still in Bull's Creek?'

Brad shrugged. 'When I got my horse from the livery barn, the ostler told me there were six strangers in town. He said they'd come from the east. I reckon that must be them.'

'They still in town?'

'They were when I left but that was over an hour ago.'

Jack seemed agitated. He strode through the snow to the trail where his horse stood waiting. The animal had doubled back on itself after bolting along the trail and catching Brad's attention. Jack swung himself into the saddle. 'How far to town?' he asked.

Brad untethered his pinto. 'About an hour's easy riding.'

'How long if I push it?'

'Wait a minute,' Brad said as he swung onto his horse. 'I'm coming with you.'

'This doesn't concern you,' Jack said.

'Bull's Creek is my town. If those men are outlaws and they're in my town, then it's my job to deal with them. What have they done, anyhow?'

'There's no time,' Jack said. 'I've got the details in my saddle-bag, along with warrants for the arrests of those men. We've got to get to town. I'll explain when we get there.' He set off along the trail at a gallop.

'Damn,' Brad hissed. He spurred the pinto into a gallop and chased after the black marshal. He had finally got his wish for excitement. But he would prefer to know exactly what he was getting himself into.

All thoughts of his family forgotten for the moment, he raced along the snowy trail towards the unknown.

# 4

As they reached town, the wind had begun to howl, kicking up powdery snow and blowing it in wind-whipped shapes along the main street like scattering ghosts. Brad led the way to Josh Gibson's livery barn. He felt a mixture of excitement and nervousness as they entered town. This morning, at the funeral, he had longed for a break in the monotony of his life in Bull's Creek. Now that break had come in the form of Dyer and his men, Brad wondered if he wasn't too old for all of this.

He was thirty-four, which was not old by anyone's standards and he kept himself relatively fit. He didn't feel old. But he had reminded himself during the ride back to town that he hadn't fired the Colt Navy in his holster in a good many years except for target practice. Now, he might be required to save his or someone else's life with the gun. He wasn't sure if he was up to it.

He slid from the saddle and Jack did likewise. They led the horses into the livery barn.

Josh was forking hay into the stalls as the two men entered. 'Sheriff,' he said, nodding. 'Did you manage to find a clear trail?'

Brad nodded. 'Josh, you know those six fellers who rode in last night?'

'Uh-huh.'

'They still in town?'

The ostler shook his head. 'No, sheriff. They lit out a while ago. Well, four of 'em did anyhow.'

'Only four?' Jack asked.

Josh glanced at Jack then looked back to Brad. 'Two of 'em stayed behind,' he said. 'I think I heard 'em say they was waitin' for someone.'

'That'd be me,' Jack told Brad. 'They must have realized Joe Bragg failed to stop me, so this time two of them have stayed behind to do the job.'

'I think you're right,' Brad said. 'Josh, do you know where these two fellers are at?'

The ostler scratched his chin and seemed to be searching for a memory. 'I think I heard 'em say they was goin' back to the saloon.'

'That'd make sense,' Brad said. 'The saloon looks out over the main street so they could watch for you coming into town.'

'Well they won't have to wait long,' Jack said, heading for the barn door.

'Wait,' Brad said, staying the black man with a hand on his shoulder. 'Before I get involved in any shooting, I want you to come back to my office and tell me what this is all about. Those fellers ain't going anywhere.'

Jack seemed to consider this, then nodded. 'All right.'

'We'll get to my office by the back alleys. That way they won't know you're in town and we'll have the advantage of surprise. Josh, can you see to our horses and let us out your back way?'

Jack removed a small saddle-bag and slung it over his shoulder. Josh led them out back where a couple of horses were exercising in his corral. Brad and Jack skirted the fence to an alley behind the main street buildings. Brad led the way.

They reached a side alley and Brad led Jack along it. 'My office doesn't have a back door,' he told Jack. 'We'll have to walk out on to the street and go in the front way.'

'That'll be OK,' Jack replied. 'Those fellers don't know what I look like. They'll be looking for a rider entering town. Probably won't notice us.'

Brad nodded and they walked on to the main street, turned left on to the boardwalk and made their way to the law office.

Once inside, they removed their coats and hats and Brad stoked up the stove. As Brad made coffee, he watched Jack stare out of the window at the Bull's

Head Saloon down the main drag. 'That the town's only saloon?' Jack asked.

'Yeah, they'll be in there watching the street.' He relaxed in his chair and placed the steaming mugs of coffee on his desk. 'Now you can tell me what the hell this is all about.'

Jack picked up the saddle-bag he had removed from his horse and opened it. He emptied the contents over the desk. Brad looked at the papers.

'Warrants,' Jack said. 'For the arrests of seven men. Joe Bragg, Henry Ward, Clem and Jud Barker, Pete Wilks, Jeff Turner and John Dyer.' He laid out drawings of six of the men over the warrants. Brad noticed something flash in Jack's eyes as he held Dyer's picture in his damaged right hand. 'Dyer is the leader,' he told Brad, laying the picture down.

Brad looked it all over. But something didn't seem right about all of this. 'How come you're chasing them on your own?'

'The marshal's office has given me a month to bring these men to justice. If I fail, they'll get others on the case.'

'Why are you so special that they're giving you this time to try to catch them on your own? After all, there must be a price on these fellers' heads. A lot of men would take up the hunt if the price was right. So why you?'

Jack looked calmly into Brad's eyes. 'Me and Dyer have got a reckoning coming. I know someone with some influence in the marshal's office. He arranged this for me.'

Brad considered. 'What do you mean you and Dyer have got a reckoning?'

Jack held up his damaged right hand. 'He did this to me a long time ago. I had to learn to do everything over again, left-handed.'

'So the marshal's office has given you the job of catching him just because he shot up your hand? I don't buy it, Jack.'

Jack turned back to the window. 'There's more to it than that,' he said slowly. 'The man who arranged this, the man in the marshal's office, he's John Dyer's father.'

Brad shook his head slowly and looked at the pictures and warrants on his desk. 'OK, I can believe that the old man might want his son stopped. After all, if he works in the marshal's office, having a son who's an outlaw has to be an embarrassment at the least. But that still doesn't explain why he's sent *you*. Out of all the gunmen in this country. Why you?'

'Because his father knows I can beat him,' Jack said, pointing to the picture of Dyer.

'And how could he know that?'

Jack remained silent. He moved to the window and stared out at the snow-covered town.

'There's a hell of a lot you're not telling me,' Brad surmised. 'Yet you expect me to go over to that saloon with you and back you up when you go against those two men.'

'You don't have to,' Jack said as he

watched the saloon. The fingers of his left hand stroked the butt of his gun lightly. 'I'm not going to ask you to. I'll go alone.'

'And I'm supposed to sit here behind my desk and let you go over there on your own?'

Jack shrugged.

Brad sighed and reached for the papers on John Dyer. He just didn't know how to play this. He knew Jack Hart wasn't telling him the whole story. But on the other hand, the black man was a deputy US marshal and it was Brad's job to help him if he required it. He scanned the marshal office's record of John Dyer with half-interest until his eyes fell upon a name that made him sit bolt upright in his chair and stare at the document in disbelief.

Jack said something from the window but Brad didn't hear it. He felt the breath hiss out of him as if he had been punched. His arms and legs went weak and he dropped the paper. He heard someone say 'Oh my God' and realized it was his own voice as he pushed up from his chair. He needed some air. Staggering away from the desk, he knocked over his mug of coffee. The hot liquid spread over the papers and Brad was dimly aware of Jack retrieving them from the desk and asking him if he was OK. The mug fell to the floor and shattered into tiny shards. Brad made for the door. He felt sick.

He wrenched open the door and a blast of icy wind hit his face, bringing him around. He stood there, hands on his knees, bent over, dimly aware of the townsfolk watching him with curiosity.

He felt a hand on his shoulder and Jack guided him back into the office, closing out the wind. 'Brad,' the black man said worriedly. 'What's the matter?' He sat Brad down in the chair behind the desk.

Brad felt himself shaking as he pointed to the paper he had been reading on Dyer. 'Wyoming,' he whispered. He couldn't trust himself to speak louder in case his voice cracked and he broke down. 'Wyoming, 1869.' He put his face in his hands as Jack picked up the paper and read aloud.

'Wyoming, 1869,' Jack read. 'Dyer, Ward and Turner held up the bank at Little Springs, Wyoming. They escaped with a little over four thousand dollars, killing three bank clerks in the process. In the ensuing gun battle on the streets before Dyer and his men fled, two town citizens were caught in the crossfire and killed: George Campbell and Edna Harris.'

Brad looked up at the black marshal. 'Edna Harris was my mother,' he said. Saying the words released something within him and he wept. A mixture of bad emotion swept through him: sorrow at the loss of his mother; anger because she had been dead ten years and he hadn't known; and guilt because if he had gone home after the war, he would have known her for four years before she had been killed. He would have been there. But instead, he had been drifting around the country, fleeing the rigid discipline of his father.

Jack came over to the desk quietly. 'Sheriff, I've been on Dyer's trail for five days now and I've seen the suffering he leaves behind him wherever he goes. That's why I've got to stop him.'

Brad wiped his eyes and stood up. 'I'm coming with you, Jack.'

'To the saloon?'

Brad nodded. 'To the saloon. Then on to Dyer's trail.'

Jack frowned. 'Brad, I don't know . . . '

'I want him, Jack!'

Jack checked his Peacemaker. 'First let's get over to the saloon and deal with the immediate problem.'

Brad nodded and checked his own weapon. 'I'll go in through the back way. You go in the front. I've seen the pictures so we shouldn't have any trouble recognizing these two fellers.'

Jack put his coat and hat on. 'You're sure about this? I could go alone.'

Brad thought of his mother. He thought of his father and he thought of Laura. 'I'm sure,' he said.

'All right.' Jack went out on to the street and started for the saloon.

Brad put on his coat, pressed his hat to his head, and headed for the alley which led around the back of the Bull's Head.

He knew he had to remain calm if he was going to get involved in a gunfight but he felt as if his body was on fire with anger at these men who could take life away without remorse and tear up families without a second thought.

The anger swelling up within him made him shake and he fought desperately in an effort to control it.

He couldn't.

They had killed his mother.

And they were going to pay.

# 5

Jack strode on to the boardwalk in front of the saloon and waited until Brad had slipped out of sight behind the building before going in through the batwings.

The Bull's Head was full. The smoky air clawed at Jack's throat as he walked to the bar, scanning the patrons seated in the room. A pianist plinked at an old piano in the corner and the sound of raucous laughter filled the saloon. Jack stood at the bar until the bartender came over.

'Whiskey,' Jack said.

The bartender took a bottle and filled a shot glass, sliding it across the scarred wood of the bar to Jack.

'Hey, bartender,' came an angry shout from somewhere in the room. 'You ain't serving him, are ya?'

The bartender shrugged as he took Jack's money. 'I don't see why not.'

The feller who had shouted came over to the bar and stood facing Jack. Jack turned and recognized the red-haired man as Pete Wilks. Wilks was staring at him angrily. Jack returned the stare.

'What's yer name, feller?' Wilks asked. The laughter in the room had ceased as everyone stopped to listen to the exchange. The atmosphere in the room had become threatening.

'Jack.'

Wilks thought for a moment then laughed cruelly. 'Jack. Black Jack. You like to play blackjack, Black Jack?'

Jack said nothing. He downed his whiskey.

'I'm talkin' to ya,' Wilks shouted.

The bartender looked pale. 'Come on, mister,' he said to Wilks, 'I don't want no trouble in my place.'

Wilks looked at him and sneered, 'Then you shouldn't have served this feller,' he said, as he jerked a thumb at Jack. 'We don't want to drink with his kind.'

Jack controlled the anger that threatened to rise within him. If he let it build up, it would cloud his judgement. He needed to stay calm.

Wilks turned to the other customers. 'We don't want his type here do we, folks?'

'Shut up, Wilks,' Jack said softly.

Wilks spun around to face Jack again. His face oozed anger and managed to look surprised at the same time. 'How the hell do you know my name, mister?'

Jack said nothing. He remained calm while Wilks got angrier and more out of control. That meant that when it came time to use his gun, Jack would have the advantage of clear thinking.

'Wait a minute,' Wilks said, thinking hard. 'Are you the feller been following us for the past five days? Goddammit! Jeff, it's him. It's the feller we been waitin' for!'

A short, dark-haired man with a beard stood up from a table near the back of the room. Jeff Turner.

'Just who the hell are you, mister?' Wilks spat. 'Why you been following us?'

'Don't you know me?' Jack asked calmly.

Wilks studied his face closely. 'I ain't never seen you before in my life, mister. Jeff, you know this feller?'

Jeff came closer. 'No,' he said. 'I'd remember a son of a bitch like him.'

'We don't know who the hell you are,' Wilks said. 'But we know you been following us. So we're gonna stop ya.'

'Like Joe Bragg stopped me?'

Wilks sneered, 'Joe always was soft. Nothing like us, mister. We're gonna do the job proper.'

The bartender edged along the bar as he saw what was coming. Half of the saloon's occupants rushed out the door. The others took cover behind tables. The bartender disappeared behind the bar. Only Jack, Wilks and Turner remained standing. The atmosphere in the smoky saloon became tense.

Jack whipped his long coat behind his holster. He let his left hand hang loosely near the butt of the Peacemaker.

Wilks seemed confused when he saw Jack's holster on his left hip then glanced at Jack's right hand. His jaw hung open and he visibly paled. He looked into Jack's eyes. 'I don't believe it. It's *you*.'

★ ★ ★

Brad watched through the kitchen door, still shaking. He gripped his Navy Colt tightly. He could sense he would need it soon. The atmosphere was thick with tension. Jack and Wilks were squared off by the bar with Turner slowly moving around the room so that he could flank Jack. Brad decided that when it came down to it, he would take out Turner. Jack would have to beat Wilks. They were too close for Brad to risk a shot in their direction. He opened the door slightly, wincing as it creaked in protest.

That one small sound was enough to break the tension in the room. Jack, Wilks and Turner all went for their guns at the same time. Brad leapt through the doorway and let off a shot at Turner. It went wide and hit the table to Turner's left. Wood chips fountained into the air. Turner spun around, noticed Brad and drew his gun from his hip.

Before he had a chance to fire it, a shot rang out from the bar and Brad noticed Wilks twist away from Jack and collide with a bar stool. The stool smashed as Wilks's body fell heavily upon it. Wilks, holding a hand to his bloody chest, fired. The bullet went into the floorboards. Wilks hit the floor in a heap and didn't move again.

Turner got his shot off and Brad heard it tear into the wall above him. He raised his Navy for a second try but Turner was already crumpling to the floor, the echo of a second shot from Jack's Peacemaker ringing around the room. Jack stood calmly at the bar, his gun smoking.

Brad surveyed the scene. The saloon's customers came out of hiding, chattering excitedly among themselves. The bartender reappeared from behind the bar, wiping sweat from his forehead. Brad approached Jack. The black marshal holstered his Colt and Brad did likewise.

'Thanks,' Brad said. 'You may have just saved my life.'

'May have?' Jack asked, grinning.

'Let me buy you a drink.'

They took their whiskies to a corner table while someone went to fetch the undertaker. 'What was all that about?' Brad asked.

'What?'

'That Wilks feller seemed to recognize you.'

Jack shrugged and took a slug of whiskey.

Brad looked at the bodies on the floor. 'Jack, what's your connection with these fellers?'

'None. Dyer must have told them about me at some time.'

'So what's your connection with him?'

'I told you. We go back a'ways.' Jack said the words with a finality that made Brad decide not to press the matter further.

Instead, he said, 'So are we gonna pick up Dyer's trail in the morning?'

Jack shook his head. 'There's no time. It looks like it may snow again tonight. I've got to get on the trail immediately.'

'I'm coming with you,' Brad said adamantly.

'I'm not so sure I want you to.'

'Look,' Brad said, 'I know I didn't perform too well just now. I've been sheriff of this backwater town so long, I haven't fired my gun in a real situation for a long time. But I used to be good. It'll come back. All I need is some time.' He wondered if he was so desperate to leave Bull's Creek that he would rather risk his life than stay. But he realized it was more than his desire to leave that spurred him on: these men had killed his mother.

'Time is one thing we don't have,' Jack replied. 'The next time you have to draw that gun, it could be Dyer you're up against. There's no way you could beat him. No way.'

'He killed my mother,' Brad said softly. 'I'd die trying.'

Jack sighed. 'Look, Brad, I know how you feel. But I can't let you come along. Yesterday I had a seventeen-year-old kid asking me the same thing because Dyer shot his father. Seventeen, Brad. Barely old enough to shave yet he wanted to kill a man. I told him no for the same reason I'm telling you no: you'll get yourself killed. You can't beat him.'

'But you can, of course,' Brad said sarcastically.

Jack looked him in the eyes and nodded. 'Yes, I can.'

Brad felt frustrated at this man with his statements shrouded in mystery.

'Look, I'm going to ask you a question and I want a straight answer from you. How the hell do you know you can beat John Dyer in a gunfight?'

Jack knocked back his drink. He looked at Brad squarely and said evenly, 'Because I've beaten him at least a hundred times before.'

# 6

'What the hell did you mean by that?' Brad demanded, as he followed Jack out of the saloon. He had had enough of this man and his mysterious statements. He wanted to know exactly what was going on. 'What do you mean you've beaten him before?'

'I don't have time to explain,' Jack said glancing at the mountains. 'There's another storm coming and I've got to get on Dyer's trail before the snow comes down.' He headed across the street toward the livery barn.

'Wait,' Brad said, 'I'm coming with you.'

'No,' Jack said, shaking his head. 'I don't have time to wait for you.'

'I won't be long,' Brad said. 'I just need to get some supplies from the store.' He pointed down the street.

Jack shook his head. 'I don't have time.'

Brad followed the black man into the barn. 'I'm coming,' he said, as Jack started to cinch the saddle to the black stallion. 'That man killed my mother. Hell, I've got more reason to want him than you do.'

Jack buckled the harness on his saddle. 'No you don't,' he said matter-of-factly.

Brad looked at him closely. 'Just what is your connection to Dyer?'

'I don't have time,' Jack said, as he led his horse out into the street. He pointed at the mountains. Angry black clouds swarmed over the rocky peaks. 'I'm heading west,' he said. 'Dyer's been moving steadily west for a while. If you can get riding before that storm hits town, you might be able to catch up with me. My trail won't be hard to follow. But if you can't beat that storm, don't even try it.' He swung up on to the stallion. 'West,' he reminded Brad and started out of town.

Brad stood watching Jack disappear in the distance. He looked at the stormclouds coming over the mountains. He was sure he could keep ahead of the storm if he rode hard. But he felt guilty about leaving town. He was the sheriff. Sure, there was hardly any trouble in Bull's Creek but if there was, Brad was expected to be there. It was his duty. He hesitated, unsure.

He looked around the town where he had spent seven years of his life. He glanced toward the hill where he had stood that morning. The cemetery. Hell, he was decided.

He strode purposely toward the general store. He would need some supplies for the ride ahead of him.

This morning, he had stood in the cemetery and asked himself the question he had been asking ever since he had found the picture of his family: *do I belong here?*

Now, deep down within him, on an instinctive level, Brad knew the answer: *no*.

He had found nothing he had been searching for here. Something within him wouldn't let him settle in Bull's Creek.

He headed into the general store. It shouldn't take him long to pick up Jack's trail. After they had found Dyer, Brad wouldn't be coming back to Bull's Creek. He planned to head for Wyoming and see his father and sister. Maybe it wasn't too late to patch up old wounds. As he chose the equipment he would need for his ride, he felt as if he had suddenly stepped out of heavy shackles. As he took his purchases to the counter, he was even smiling.

Outside, the wind started to keen angrily and the dark storm swept down out of the mountains.

\* \* \*

As Kate Donnelley guided the buggy along the mountain trail, she tried to ignore the fear that gnawed at her. The storm is still some distance away, she tried to reassure herself. We'll make it home. She had been into town with her son, Patrick, who was now snuggled up against her in the rattling trap. The two horses pulling them along were the finest from their farm but even they were having difficulty in the slippery snow.

The buggy was loaded with feed from the store in Bull's Creek and Kate worried that she might have overloaded it. The wheels slid on the snow and the small trap weaved from side to side as they followed the trail which led to their farm. With the storm brewing in the mountains, she couldn't afford to be stuck out in the open if a wheel broke.

'Mummy, I'm cold,' Patrick said. He was wrapped in a knitted hat, scarf and gloves but Kate could feel him trembling against her. She wondered if his trembling might actually be because he could sense her fear. She was sure they were going to overturn.

She pulled on the reins to slow the

horses. The animals seemed desperate to reach the farm. Kate knew they could sense the big storm coming down from the mountains. We're not going to make it, she told herself. 'We'll soon be home,' she told Patrick. She tried to sound confident but she was sure the child could hear the fear in her voice. She could swear she could feel the storm in her bones. The sky seemed to become heavy and oppressing. She could smell a metallic tang in the air.

The horses started to increase their speed, the tack and harness jangling like shattered glass. Kate pulled back on the reins but the animals ignored the command to slow down. A primal fear of the storm had blinded them to anything except escape.

Kate felt Patrick put his arms around her. 'I'm scared, Mummy.'

She fought with the reins but the horses broke into a panicked dash, spraying cold snow over Kate and her son. The trap skidded and weaved crazily behind the two frightened animals. Kate heard a splintering sound from the right wheel.

She wondered if they would be safer if they jumped down out of the buggy but quickly forgot the idea. The trees on either side of the trail were rushing by; they were going too fast to jump out safely. They would have to hang on and pray for the best.

The splintering sound from the right wheel grew louder.

'I'm scared,' Patrick repeated.

The horses increased their speed.

Kate let go of the reins — there was no point holding on to them — and hugged her son tightly. 'We'll be all right,' she whispered. She wasn't sure if she was reassuring her son or herself. She hoped it wasn't herself because she didn't believe a word of what she was saying.

The buggy slid to the left and scraped against a pine tree with a loud screech of wood against wood. Splintered bark showered over them and Kate held Patrick tighter. The buggy slid back across the trail to the right and the wheel protested angrily with a shrill *crack*.

'Hold me tight,' Kate shouted at her son as she realized the wheel was going to break.

The trap skidded toward the trees on the right side of the trail and Kate braced herself for the impact. But before they reached the big pine, the wheel tore in two and snapped. The right side of the buggy dropped to the ground and a burst of cold snow fountained over Kate and Patrick.

The heavy feed bags loaded in the rear tipped out into the snow, some breaking and spilling their contents. The dropped edge of the buggy hit a rock and Kate felt it lift as the buggy overturned. She screamed but the sound was drowned out by the cracking of the wooden trap as it flipped over.

In a flurry of wet snow, spilled grain and splintered wood, the buggy landed upside down and stopped. The horses didn't have the strength to pull the overturned vehicle. They stood quietly, unable to flee the approaching storm.

Kate pulled herself and her son out from under the upturned buggy. She felt bruised but she was sure she hadn't broken anything. Patrick was crying but he seemed all right. Kate stood and looked back the way they had come. Bright yellow grain and bits of wood littered the trail.

We were lucky, she told herself. It could have been a lot worse.

Patrick walked up to her and threw his arms around her waist. 'Don't cry, Mummy,' he said softly.

Kate touched her cheek and realized she was crying. She hadn't even noticed.

'Will we still be home soon?' Patrick asked.

Kate looked at the ruins of the buggy. There was no way she could fix it before the storm started. Already the woods were getting dark as the snow clouds began to spread over them.

'I'm cold,' Patrick said.

Kate suddenly became aware of how cold she felt as well. She wore a thick long coat — one of Joe's — but beneath that she only had a thin shirt and pants on. She hadn't expected to be long in town.

She had to admit it, she didn't know what to do.

Patrick started crying again.

Maybe if we took shelter under the buggy. No, they would freeze to death. The temperature had begun to plummet and there was no way the buggy would offer enough shelter from the wind.

'I wish Daddy was here,' Patrick said through his tears.

'I know you do,' she said. But she had to admit that she was glad Joe wasn't here. He had been dead two years now, since Patrick was four, and as a husband he had been useless. They had married in Ireland eight years ago, when Kate was only nineteen and (she could now admit) naive.

Joe had promised her a life full of opportunity in America, the new land, and they had emigrated full of hope and expectation.

Kate's expectations, however, had been destroyed during their first year of marriage. She loved the country and the farm they bought but her husband had turned out to be far from the man she thought he was. Back in Ireland, he had worked as a cobbler in his father's shop and his fancy words about wanting more had been just that: words. Once they had reached America, Joe had been overwhelmed by the country. The qualities needed to live life out here — strength of character, determination and stubbornness — simply weren't part of his make-up. He had almost run their farm into the ground before Kate had taken over during the bout of pneumonia that had eventually killed him.

And when she had taken over the running of the farm, she found those qualities that Joe had lacked, within herself. She hadn't suspected they were there but after a year of running the farm, it was obvious that she was no longer the timid Irish girl who had come to America hanging on her husband's words and promises of a good life. She was now a strong, independent woman ready to carve that good life for herself. If she was honest with herself, and she usually was, she had to admit that Joe's death didn't bother her as much as she thought it would.

Remembering her past struggles strengthened Kate. She had come this far, she wouldn't give up now. She looked at the overturned buggy. She looked at the horses. She looked at the darkening woods. Shelter. They needed shelter to wait out the storm.

She sat on the upturned trap and thought. Patrick sat beside her and watched her. 'Mummy, are we lost?'

'Ssshh!' Kate hissed at her son. She had heard something in the woods. She placed a finger to her lips to keep

Patrick quiet. She strained to hear the sound again. It was faint but she could make out a muffled rushing sound. She took her son's hand and started into the woods on the right side of the trail.

The snow reached Patrick's knees and hidden undergrowth snagged their feet as they made their way through the trees. Kate stopped and listened. The rushing sound was louder. She picked Patrick up and increased her pace toward the source of the sound. Just as the snow began to tumble to earth, she found what she had been searching for.

The river.

A thick layer of ice covered the moving water and the crystalline covering muffled the sound of the river. Usually, the deep flowing water could be heard clearly from the trail. Kate wondered if the small waterfall downriver had frozen over. Last winter, she had taken Patrick there and they had marvelled at the cascading ice shapes. That was when they had discovered the cabin.

On the other side of the river, deep in the woods, someone had built a small log cabin. It was abandoned now but it would still offer shelter and warmth to Kate and Patrick.

But they had to cross the river to get to it.

Kate wondered if the ice would support their weight.

Last winter, she and Patrick had played on the ice. But that had been in the middle of winter when the ice was thick. Winter was only just beginning to spread over the woods now and the ice would be unstable, dangerous.

A blast of cold wind iced through her as she stood at the edge of the frozen river. She looked at Patrick shivering beside her. We've got to get across. We need warmth and shelter. Taking her son's hand, she stepped tentatively on to the ice.

A soft crackling sound spread across the glassy surface as her weight pressed down on it. Kate stopped, waited until Patrick had moved beside her, then took another step. The ice creaked.

She had to fight the urge to run across to the far bank. Her nerves were taut as she stood on the crackling ice and forced herself to go slowly and steadily. If she lost her nerve and ran, if her footfalls became too heavy, if she went into the icy water of the river, they were as good as dead.

They progressed slowly to the centre of the river. At the halfway point, Kate halted and tried to calm herself. Sweat bathed her body and she was trembling. 'Nearly there,' she whispered to Patrick. She realized that speaking out loud couldn't cause the ice beneath their feet to crack open and swallow them but even though she knew she was being ridiculous, she couldn't bring herself to speak louder than a whisper.

Patrick remained silent, as if he might be having the same thoughts as his mother.

They stepped forward once more, listening to the ice creak and moan around them, aware of the deep, cold, moving water beneath them.

Thick snow came at them on the freezing wind. The white maelstrom whipped at their faces, blinding them. Kate pulled Patrick's scarf up over his face and, shielding her eyes with her hand, led them the rest of the way across the river. As they stepped on to the far bank, she let out a sigh of relief. They weren't far from the old cabin now. She picked Patrick up and started to push through the trees and bushes away from the river. Within the sheltering wood, the snow fell lighter.

Kate stopped and crouched low when she heard a sound in the trees to her left. A harsh, man's laugh. Peering over a tangle of bushes, she could make out two men moving down to the river. Who were they? Had they seen her crossing over the ice? What were they doing out here?

She crept further along and kept low. She didn't know why but something inside her told her not to let these men see her. She waited until she was well out of sight before she stood up straight again.

She walked carefully toward the cabin.

Then, when she heard shots ring out from the direction of the river, she ran.

# 7

When Jack found the overturned buggy on the trail, he became worried. The horses regarded him steadily as he inspected the remains of the shattered trap. He knew Dyer had come this way; Jack had picked up his trail some time ago. If the outlaw and his men were responsible for this destruction, it would mean the death count had risen again. Jack scanned the nearby snow but the storm had arrived in full force now and deep fresh snow obscured any tracks that might tell him what had happened here.

He unhitched the two horses from the buggy and led them into the sheltering pine trees. He tethered them to a stout branch and tied his own horse alongside them. He couldn't go any further while the snow whipped down so he decided to rest in the woods. He sat on a fallen log and removed his hat, shaking the snow off it.

He wondered at Dyer's motives. The man seemed to be moving steadily west at a good pace, as if he had some place to get to. And in his wake, he left a trail of destruction. Jack thought of Liz Carlson, left to bring up Todd and Ethan on her own now that Dyer had killed their father. He thought of Brad Harris's shock when he had discovered his mother had been killed by Dyer's gang in Wyoming. He thought of his own father in Colorado. He looked at his nearly useless right hand. He thought of his brother.

Whenever Jack thought of his brother, one memory always stood out clearest in his mind. The pond.

Jack had been ten, his brother, Richard, twelve, and they played frequently near the pond on their father's land in Colorado. The deep, silvery water fascinated the two boys and they would dare each other to jump from the bank on to a partially submerged rock then from that rock to a smaller one further out. On the hot summer's day that now stuck out in Jack's mind so clearly, his brother leapt on to the first rock and then out on to the second while Jack sat in the grass on the bank. Richard danced around on the small rock in the pond, the sunlight reflected off the water flickering over him and making him appear ghost-like. 'Jack,' he called. 'I'm going to go further than you.' He pointed to a rock near the middle of the deep pond.

Jack had seen that rock before but had never considered jumping on to it. It was too far and too small, the water surrounding it too deep. He shook his head. 'Don't be an idiot, you'll never make it.'

His brother stopped dancing around and looked serious. 'I'll show you who's the idiot,' he shouted. 'You're just afeared and you don't want me to make it 'cos I'll be better than you.'

'No,' Jack said, as he stood up. He

felt a knot of fear in his stomach.

'Come on, this isn't fun any more. Let's go and play at gunfights or pretend we're cowboys on the range.'

Richard shook his head. 'No, you're always better than me at those things. Well this time, I'm gonna be better than you. Watch.' He turned to face the rock in the shimmering pond and bent his legs, ready to jump.

'No!' Jack shouted. But it was too late. His brother had sprung out toward the rock. He landed on it with one foot but his other slipped into the pond. He screamed and toppled into the deep water with a loud splash.

His screams were cut off as he hit the water but Jack's continued to pierce the summer day's heat. He leapt on to the first two rocks then, without thinking, toward the rock his brother had fallen from. Maybe it was because he was smaller and lighter than his tall, lanky brother or maybe it was because he was charged with adrenalin but Jack made the jump. When his brother surfaced, splashing and gurgling, Jack made a grab for his shirt. He missed and Richard went under again.

Panicking, Jack lunged forward and pushed his arm underwater, groping frantically in the cool water. His searching fingers met nothing but weeds.

Richard had been under for too long.

Jack couldn't swim any more than his brother could. He jumped back toward the shore and splashed through the shallower water there until he reached the bank. He started to run to his pa in the ranch house. When he saw the house in the distance, he stopped. He could never make it there and back in time. By the time he returned with his pa, Richard would be drowned.

Jack sprinted into the trees by the pond and searched frantically around until he found a long branch. Returning to the water, he wondered if it was already too late for his brother. Not allowing himself to dwell on that thought, he leapt back to the rock Richard had fallen from and started prodding the branch into the deep water. He touched the bottom and realized how deep the pond was. He continued his search until he prodded something soft.

Richard! Jack felt his heart jump. He had found his brother. But how long had it been since Richard had last breathed air? Jack had lost all sense of time. He gripped the branch tightly and pushed its end toward the shallower water near the pond's edge. He felt the heavy weight on the end drift through the water out of the depths.

When he had manoeuvred Richard into the shallows, Jack leapt from the rock and waded to the shallows himself, grabbing his brother and pulling him towards the bank.

Richard lay still in the grass, eyes closed, water streaming from his nostrils and mouth. 'Richard,' Jack whispered. 'Richard.'

His brother didn't respond.

'Richard!' Jack cried, shaking his brother. Richard's head lolled loosely around, pond water spraying from his mouth.

Then he coughed.

Jack started crying with relief. Richard was alive.

His brother spluttered and coughed again, expelling the water from his lungs. He collapsed onto his stomach and lay panting.

'Richard,' Jack said. 'Are you OK?'

Richard remained still, breathing steadily but not moving. His eyes were still closed.

Jack ran for the ranch house to fetch his pa.

Jack watched the snow fall silently through the trees. That day at the pond all those years ago was the last good time he and Richard had spent together. From the moment he had pulled his brother out of the water, everything had turned sour. Richard had been underwater too long, the doctor told Jack and his father. He had gone too long without air and it had damaged his brain.

After that, everything had flipped crazily.

And now, Richard was gone.

Nothing could bring his brother back now. Dyer had seen to that. Jack held up his right hand, the hand he had used to drag his brother out of the pond. Destroyed by Dyer.

He started suddenly, alerted by a sound coming through the trees. Drawing the Peacemaker, he crouched in the snow and listened intently to the woods around him.

It came again, the steady crunching of someone walking through the snow. Jack gently cocked the Peacemaker, wincing as the hammer locked into place with a loud *click*.

The footsteps came closer, approaching from the direction of the trail.

Jack found cover behind the fallen log he had been sitting on. The horses, sensing the presence of a stranger, whinnied.

The footsteps ceased, as if the intruder had heard the sound.

A whisper came floating on the cold air. 'Jack?'

Jack stayed low. 'Brad?' he hissed.

Brad came out of the trees, his Colt Navy revolver levelled at his hip.

Jack stood up. He wasn't sure if he was glad to see the lawman or not. He had half-hoped Brad wouldn't follow him. But part of him was glad of the help. Dyer had three men with him and those odds weren't good. Besides, Jack guessed Brad had a right to be there because of what had happened to his mother.

'I found the buggy,' Brad explained, knocking snow from his hat. 'I followed your tracks from there.' He hitched his horse with the other three. 'You seen Dyer and his men?'

Jack shook his head. 'He can't be far. The storm will have slowed him some.'

'Well,' Brad said, 'there's worse coming. The sky back there' — he pointed the way he had come — 'is turning black. I've never seen anything like it.'

'We'll need to find some shelter.'

'There's an old trapper's cabin beyond the river,' Brad said. 'If the river's frozen over, we could hole up in there until the worst of the storm passes.'

Jack considered this and nodded. 'Sounds good.' He started to untie the horses then stopped and jumped for cover as a shot rang out through the trees. Brad dropped to the ground, looking around frantically, Colt ready.

Another shot came from the same direction followed by a barking laugh. 'You missed him, Pa.'

'Shut up, Clem,' came the angry reply. 'Goddamn jack-rabbit. I nearly got the critter.'

'It's Clem and Jud Barker,' Jack whispered to Brad.

'Sounds like they're near the river,' Brad whispered back.

Leaving the horses, they split up,

Jack swinging through the trees to the left while Brad took the right.

Jack reached the bank of the frozen river and peered through the snow. With the absence of trees over the river, Jack could see the black sky Brad had warned him about. There was one hell of a storm coming. He heard a sound to his right and swung round, the Peacemaker drawn and ready. But it was only Brad further downriver.

A sudden noise across the ice alerted Jack and he sank back into the shadow of the trees as Jud Barker appeared on the opposite bank brandishing a shotgun. He was old and Jack knew he had been on the wrong side of the law nearly all his life. 'Where the hell is that goddamn critter?' he snarled.

Clem came out of the trees laughing. His appearance bore a strong resemblance to his father's except Clem's straggly hair was brown while Jud's had turned white. 'That rabbit's clear gone by now, Pa,' Clem said.

'Shaddap,' Jud snapped back. He

continued searching the snowy undergrowth near the river for the rabbit he
had missed with the shotgun.

Jack watched from the trees, wondering
what might be the best plan to
undertake. He didn't know if Dyer
and Henry Ward were near. He hated
being at a disadvantage like that. The
odds were too unpredictable. He cursed
and watched the outlaws searching the
trees across the frozen river.

His decision was made for him when
a shot from his right made him jump.

Brad had fired. Jud Barker also
jumped but the cause of his action
was not surprise; he had caught a bullet
in his gut. He yelped and collapsed
to the snow screaming. 'Goddamn it,'
Jack hissed to himself. The die was
cast now.

Clem took a second to appraise
the situation then drew a sidearm
and started to fire across the river
indiscriminately. Brad fired again and
the bullet nicked a branch near Clem's
head. Clem dived into the trees for

cover. Jud continued to scream. He sounded like he was in a lot of pain.

Shots came from the undergrowth where Clem had hidden himself, all aimed in Brad's direction. Jack levelled the Peacemaker and it thundered as he squeezed the trigger. Clem started to fire back at him and Jack moved to his left, keeping low as he moved along the riverbank. If he could move upriver and get across the ice, he could get behind Clem. While the shooting continued behind him and Jud continued screaming, he wound through the trees and down to the iced river.

He stepped on to the smooth, glassy surface and started to cross to the opposite side. Below his feet, through the clear ice, he could see the river-bed far below him. He wondered how thick the ice was. Trying to suppress the thought, he walked carefully across the river.

He had almost made it when he realized Jud Barker had stopped screaming. The old man had seen Jack and was reaching for his shotgun. Jack cursed himself. He had discounted Jud because of his wound and screaming. Now he was trapped in the open, an easy target.

Jud fired and the shotgun roared.

Jack panicked and instinctively jumped to the side to avoid the shot. Too late he realized that he would land heavily on the ice. He prayed that it was thick enough to take the impact.

He landed on his stomach and the air in his lungs shot out with a *whuff* as he winded himself. Spidery cracks crazed through the ice beneath him with a brittle crackling and Jack knew he was going through into the cold, deep waters below. He struggled for breath, knowing that holding air in his lungs wouldn't keep him alive beneath the ice; the water was so cold it would drain the warmth and life from him as soon as it enveloped him.

He grabbed a lungful of chilled air as the ice around him shattered and he plunged into a coldness which was complete and deathly.

\* \* \*

Brad saw Jack crash through the ice and knew he had to act immediately if he was going to save the black marshal's life. He drew a bead on Jud Barker and fired, killing the old outlaw. Clem, seeing his pa dead, broke cover and stood up, firing at Brad wildly. Brad levelled the Colt and squeezed off a shot which sent Clem spinning into the trees, dead.

Brad rushed upriver toward the spot Jack had gone through the ice. He ran on to the ice, searching for his friend. Below the clear ice, he could make out a dark shape moving with the river's current. Jack!

Brad didn't know if the black man was alive or dead, he only knew he had to get him out from beneath the ice. He started pounding on the frozen surface with his gun butt, trying to break through but the ice was too thick. And Jack was moving further down river.

Brad became frantic. He followed the dark shape down the river, his mind racing to find a way to free Jack from the icy tomb. He looked around desperately. There had to be some way.

An idea struck him and he sprinted toward the river bank, praying it wasn't too late.

★ ★ ★

Jack's body had spun in the water. He had entered the deathly cold water head down but now he was looking at the ice above him. As the river's insistent current dragged him along, his hands dragged along it. Beyond that glassy layer was air.

The cold of the water had shocked his system and Jack wasn't even sure if he had drowned already. His blood felt as cold as the water. He didn't know if he was still holding his breath or if his lungs were full of icy water. His mind had become slow and frozen.

I can let the current take me and forget all my worries, it told him. The pull of the river, which had at first seemed like it was trying to drag him along like a rough fighter, now seemed like the gentle tug of an insistent lover. Jack could feel himself surrendering to its iciness. He knew he had no chance of survival.

He thought of his brother and knew he had failed in his hunt for Dyer. Even that thought didn't hold any emotion for him. His thinking was frozen. He dimly remembered pulling his brother from the pond that summer long ago. So many things had changed since then. No one was going to pull him from the water. Better to let it take him easily than fight it. Maybe, he thought, his brother would have been better off if he had drowned in the pond. Then none of the later mess would have happened.

As he thought that, he felt his whole body begin to stop. The cold gripped him tightly in its deathly embrace.

★ ★ ★

Brad rode through the trees frantically, ignoring the branches as they scratched at his face. His horse weaved between the trees toward the river as Brad spurred it on as fast as he dared.

He reached the bank and spotted the dark shape drifting below the ice. He's dead already, he told himself. That water's got to be nearly freezing. Ignoring the thought, he rode the horse along the edge of the river until he was just ahead of Jack. Then, he pulled hard on the reins and shouted at his mount.

The animal jumped on to the frozen river at Brad's command and its weight combined with the force of impact as it landed broke through the ice. The animal's flanks hit the cold water and the horse whinnied, pulling itself out of the hole it had created.

Brad slid from the saddle and knelt at the edge of the hole. He looked upriver where the dark shape beneath the ice headed towards him. He plunged his arms into the freezing water, gasping at the instant numbness that spread through him. My God, he thought. There's no way he can be alive.

He groped blindly in the river as Jack's body drifted beneath him. Brad caught hold of something and pulled. His fingers and forearms were frozen and unfeeling. Gathering his strength, he heaved his body backwards, gripping Jack's coat.

Jack surfaced and Brad pulled him out of the water and on to the ice. The black man lay still, not moving, not breathing.

Brad pushed him on to his side to let the water drain from Jack's mouth. He clapped his hand hard on Jack's back in an attempt to get the black man to cough the water out of his lungs. Jack lay still.

'Goddamnit!' Brad shouted in frustration. He rolled Jack on to his stomach and pressed his back, attempting to pump the cold water out of his body. A stream of river water sprayed out of Jack's mouth and spread across the ice. Still Jack lay motionless.

Brad felt powerless. He was sure Jack was dead. No one could survive in such cold water for so long. In desperation, and because he didn't know what else to do, he pressed on Jack's back one more time.

The black marshal coughed and spluttered, rolling on to his back. Brad pushed him back onto his side. 'Let the water drain out of your throat,' he said. Then, he burst out laughing. As Jack lay on the ice, hacking and gasping for breath, a fit of laughter overcame Brad. As he bent over, his sides hurting, he realized it was his body's way of releasing the tension that had built up inside him while trying to rescue Jack. It was relief.

Because, he understood, he had come to regard the black man as his friend. Although Jack kept himself shrouded in a cloud of mystery, Brad knew instinctively that he was a good man. He knew that although Jack seemed surly at times, deep down he cared for the people who had been hurt by Dyer. He seemed to take a personal responsibility for them. Brad had an idea why this might be the case but if Jack wanted to keep his motives secret, he would respect that.

Jack had managed to get to his feet and had doubled over, hands on his knees, while he coughed out the last of the water. Brad put an arm around him and Jack leaned heavily against him.

The chill wind cut across the river like a shard of ice. 'We need to get somewhere warm,' Brad said. 'That cabin isn't too far from here.' He looked around for his pinto but the animal had fled after its plunge in the cold river. 'I'll get a fire going in the cabin then come back for the horses,' Brad told Jack.

Jack nodded weakly. 'Thanks,' he said. 'You saved my life.'

'Forget it,' Brad replied.

'Now I know how he felt when he was in the pond. So dark. So lonely.'

'How *who* felt?' Brad asked. He wondered if Jack had become delirious.

'My brother,' Jack said, as they entered the woods and headed for the cabin.

'I didn't realize you had a brother,' Brad said.

Jack was silent for a moment. Then he said slowly, 'I don't any more.'

Brad wondered if another piece of the puzzle that surrounded this black US marshal had just clicked into place.

# 8

John Dyer sat on the edge of the snow-covered rocks which thrust above the trees and watched the snow melting on the palm of his outstretched hand. Although the snow storm raged around him and the wind cut through his long black coat, he was oblivious to anything but the white flakes turning to water on his skin. He observed their changing shapes as they dissolved into the tiny puddle in his hand.

That circle of water reminded him of something he would rather forget so he tipped his hand over and watched the drops fall to the rocks below.

He heard a sound behind him and turned. Henry Ward came clambering up the rocks and stood hugging himself against the cold. 'It's freezing up here, John.'

Dyer stood up and brushed snow

from his coat. 'Is it?' he said. 'I hadn't noticed. I was just watching everything changing.'

Ward looked confused. He started to say something, then thought better of it and stayed silent.

'Don't you see?' Dyer asked, sweeping his arm around. 'A few days ago, the skies were blue, the ground dusty. Now, the storm has come and changed everything.'

Ward grunted and nodded.

'Did you find Jud and Clem?' Dyer asked.

Ward shook his head. 'I knew we shouldn't have let them two go off hunting. They're probably lost in the woods.'

Dyer shook his head. 'I don't think so.' Since losing Joe Bragg at the ranch, then Wilks and Turner at Bull's Creek, a fear had begun gnawing at his gut. 'I think that feller is still following us, Henry.'

Ward frowned. 'You think he got Jud and Clem?'

Dyer considered. 'It's possible. We don't know who this feller is but one thing we do know: he is very determined. And if he's managed to get past Joe, Pete, Jeff, Jud and Clem, we also know something else about him: he's damned good. All of our men were quick gunmen.'

'I still say Jud and Clem are lost,' Ward put in. 'I ain't heard no shots, leastways.'

Dyer shrugged. 'Maybe. But this wind would mask the sounds of gunfire.' He looked at the trees. 'We'd best go looking for Jud and Clem.'

Ward nodded and started down the rocks.

'You see what I mean about everything changing?' Dyer said.

Ward stopped and looked at him.

'Not long ago, there were seven of us,' Dyer explained. 'Now, if that feller got Jud and Clem, there's only two of us.'

Ward looked at the trees below the

rocks. 'You think he's that good?'

'It's possible,' Dyer said. 'I once knew someone who was quick enough.'

'That Jack Hart you told us about?'

Dyer nodded.

'Could this feller on our trail be him?'

Dyer shook his head. 'No. I fixed it so that he would never shoot again.'

Ward laughed mirthlessly and continued down the rocks.

Dyer looked at the winter storm. He wondered why he had thought of Jack Hart now, after all these years. The memory disturbed him, as it always did when it came into his mind to haunt him. Could this fellow on their trail be Jack? No, why would Jack come after him now?

*Revenge.* Dyer checked his weapon and dismissed the thought. Jack wouldn't be seeking revenge, not after all this time. Not revenge for his shot-up hand.

*Revenge for his brother.* Dyer felt a tight knot of fear in his belly. Of course, Jack had a brother, didn't he?

Dyer felt a blackness wash over him and shook his head to clear it. His memory contained parts which were murky, or totally blank. He was prone to blackouts. And Jack Hart's brother was one subject which his mind had tried to block out completely. Dyer knew there was something important about Jack Hart, but that time of his life was almost a total blur. It had been a bad time for him.

'Anyway,' he whispered to himself. 'It can't be Jack. It's too long ago and he can't shoot any more.' He started to clamber down the rocks to the woods.

* * *

Kate had managed to get a fire crackling in the fireplace of the log cabin and she and Patrick sat in front of its warm glow. Patrick had stopped complaining and stared into the flames silently, which Kate was thankful for. She knew he was only a young boy and had a right to be frightened but she had

118

enough to worry about thinking of the two men by the river and the gunshots she had heard.

She found herself glancing continuously at the cabin's only window. She felt afraid of what was out there in the storm. We'll be all right, she told herself. The cabin's tucked away in the trees. They won't find it. She hugged Patrick tightly, protectively. 'Warm enough?' she asked him.

The boy nodded.

Kate was aware that since his father's death, Patrick had become withdrawn. While she had emerged from that time as a stronger, more independent, person, her son had closed up some part of himself and locked it away. She wondered if the boy needed a father-figure in his life. Perhaps it was time for her to find a new man.

She wasn't only thinking of Patrick's welfare. She was a woman with a woman's needs and there were times when she longed for a man to come into her life. Not another man like Joe, of course. The woman she had turned into wouldn't tolerate another man like him. No, she realized, her standards had changed and become much higher. Perhaps too high. There had been no one else since Joe's death; no one had excited her in the ways she needed to be excited. She wondered if it was too late for her now. Had she become *too* independent and self-reliant?

A sudden movement outside the window startled her and she felt her heart lurch against her ribs. She heard movement near the door of the cabin and she grabbed Patrick, pulling him with her to the far wall. She had no weapon with which to defend herself and her son. She felt suddenly vulnerable.

The door crashed open and two men came staggering in. Kate suppressed the frightened sound which threatened to burst from her but Patrick screamed at the two intruders.

The men, one black and shivering, the other a white man supporting his companion, noticed Kate and Patrick. 'Howdy, ma'am,' the white man said, touching the brim of his hat as he lowered his companion to the floor in front of the fire.

Kate remained silent. She knew she looked scared. She wondered if she should grab Patrick and bolt through the door into the storm. She readied herself, then stopped. She recognized the man in front of her. She had seen him in town on a few occasions. She prompted her memory for his name. 'Sheriff Harris?' she said.

He nodded and removed his hat. 'That's me,' he said. 'Except I ain't sheriff any more. Please call me Brad, ma'am. And this is my friend Jack Hart.' He indicated the black man shivering in front of the fire. Jack nodded.

'You're Kate Donnelley, ain't you?' Brad asked. Kate nodded. 'Was that your buggy on the trail?'

She nodded again. 'The storm spooked my horses. They bolted up the trail and the buggy went over.' She felt her confidence returning now that she knew these men weren't a threat to her or Patrick. She didn't know much about the town's sheriff but she had heard he was a good, honest man.

He knelt so that he was level with Patrick. 'And who might you be, young man? You been looking after your mother?'

Patrick shrunk away from Brad and clung on to Kate's leg.

'He's a little scared,' Kate explained. 'We saw two men near the river and heard gunshots.'

Brad stood to face her. 'We ran into some trouble from those two fellers. Jack fell into the river.'

'My God,' Kate said as she knelt by the shivering black man. 'Are you all right?'

'Cold,' Jack said through chattering teeth.

'You'd best get out of those wet things,' she suggested. Jack nodded and started to remove his coat. Kate noticed the marshal's star pinned to his waistcoat but said nothing. She had never heard of a black marshal before but she didn't see any reason why a black man shouldn't take to a job as a lawman.

'I'll go get the horses,' Brad said. 'We've got some dry blanket rolls on the saddles. It looks like we'll be spending the night here and we'll need all the comfort we can get.' He walked to the door and opened it, letting the icy wind enter the cabin.

'Be careful,' Kate told him.

Brad looked at her, nodded, replaced his hat and walked out into the storm.

# 9

By the time Brad returned to the cabin and tethered the horses outside in the shelter of a stand of pine, he was freezing. The temperature had dropped with the onset of night. Brad had found his pinto wandering in the trees near the river and the animal seemed to have forgotten about its experiences in the water.

He removed the two saddles and hefted them over his shoulders, making sure the four horses were comfortable before he left them and entered the cabin.

Jack was sitting near the fire, his shirt removed and drying near the flames. In Kate's presence, he had kept his pants on and curls of steam rose from them as they dried in the heat from the fire. Kate and her boy sat leaning against the cabin wall, the boy holding tightly on to his mother's hand while he watched Jack closely. He looked as if he expected Jack to suddenly leap up and attack him.

Poor kid, Brad thought. Probably scared half to death. He passed Jack a dry blanket and took the other over to Kate and her son. He knelt in front of the boy and smiled at him. 'What's your name, son?'

'Patrick,' the boy said.

'Well, Patrick, this storm won't last long,' he said, trying to sound reassuring. 'By morning, you'll be back home. I bet your pa's worried about you.'

'My pa's dead,' Patrick said flatly.

Brad cursed himself silently. 'I'm sorry,' he said. He looked at Kate. 'Sorry,' he repeated.

She smiled at him and he noticed for the first time how pretty she was. Her deep-brown eyes seemed alive with an inner strength. Her soft features, framed by a cascade of tumbling red hair, did not have the fragile look Brad had seen on most of the girls in town. Kate's face bore the look of someone who had worked outdoors, on the land, most of her life. The elements had lent her face a look of rugged beauty. 'It's OK,' she said. 'You weren't to know.' For the first time, Brad noticed the Irish brogue in her voice. The accent was softened by her years in America, giving her voice a soft, lyrical quality.

Reaching inside his shirt and pulling out the silver Raven, he turned back to her son. 'Say, Patrick, has anyone ever told you the story of the Raven?'

The boy seemed entranced by the glinting metal bird hanging from its chain. He shook his head.

'It's an old Indian story,' Brad said. 'You see, the Raven had great powers but there was no one around to appreciate them. This was a long time ago, before there were any people in the world. So the Raven laid a huge egg. And with his beak, he split it open and all the people of the world came out of that egg. And you know when you see lightning in the sky?'

The boy nodded.

'Well that's the Raven flapping his wings and sending thunderbolts in his wake. That's what the Indians believe.'

Patrick watched the silver bird in Brad's hand a moment longer then turned away. For a moment, Brad had caught his interest. Now, he had lost it again. He didn't know much about kids, never having had any of his own, and he felt frustrated. He wanted to occupy the boy's thoughts, to turn his mind away from the storm raging outside, but he was out of ideas.

'Hey, Patrick,' Jack called from the fire. 'Watch this.' He removed his Peacemaker from its holster and unloaded it, putting the bullets in his pants pocket. Then he replaced the gun in its leather sheath and stood up, facing the boy. His hand became a blur and the gun appeared in it, pointing at Patrick. Jack made a shooting sound and the boy giggled, falling to the floor and playing dead.

Jack laughed and spun the gun back into the holster.

When the boy got up, Jack drew again. Brad had never seen anyone draw a gun so quickly. Jack's movements were smooth and fluid, well practised. He made the shooting sound again and the boy rolled over again then rushed over to Jack. 'Can I try it?' he asked.

Jack looked at Kate who nodded her approval. 'We'll have a shoot-out,' Jack proclaimed loudly. 'Brad, can I borrow your Colt?'

Brad unloaded the Colt and passed it to Jack. He was glad Jack had gained the boy's interest at last but he was surprised to feel a pang of jealousy. He had wanted to be the one to get Patrick to play. To please Kate? he asked himself.

Pushing the question from his mind, he sat against the log wall next to her. 'I guess I just don't have a way with kids,' he said.

'Oh, I don't know,' she replied, as Jack and Patrick squared off at opposite ends of the cabin. 'I'd say you don't have much experience with them. I thought your story about the Raven was very interesting. That amulet is lovely.'

He nodded. 'My mother and sister gave it to me when I left home to fight in the war.'

'Jack told me about your mother,' she said softly. 'I'm sorry.'

He shrugged, not knowing what to say.

'Do you think you'll catch this John Dyer?' she asked.

Brad thought of his mother. 'I certainly hope so.'

'Draw!' Jack shouted. Patrick held the heavy Peacemaker in both hands. He pointed it at Jack, who was slowly pulling Brad's Colt from his holster, letting the boy win.

'Bang!' Patrick shouted.

Jack clutched his chest as if wounded and fell to the floor. 'You got me,' he said weakly. He closed his eyes and played dead.

Patrick jumped up and down with glee. 'I got him, Mummy,' he shouted. 'I beat him at the draw!' Kate laughed and nodded, then screamed as the floorboards beneath Patrick cracked and he crashed through them.

Jack got to his feet and rushed to the hole in the boards. The boy had disappeared beneath the floor completely.

'Patrick!' Kate shouted, joining Jack at the edge of the hole.

The sounds of the boy crying came up from the darkness below. 'It's some kind of cellar,' Jack said. 'Whoever built this cabin must have dug it.'

Brad scanned the rest of the floor. 'A trap door,' he said, pointing to the edges of a door set into the floorboards. It fitted flush into the floor and had been well disguised.

Jack bent over and lifted the door open.

'Hang on,' Kate called through the hole in the old floorboards. 'We're coming, Patrick.'

'There's a ladder,' Jack said, lowering himself through the open hatch. He disappeared into the darkness and Brad could hear him calling the boy below. He glanced at Kate, sitting on the floor near the hole, her pretty face creased with worry for her son.

Jack reappeared, clambering out of the hatch with Patrick in his arms. The boy was crying softly and had dirt smeared over his face but otherwise appeared unhurt. When Jack lowered him to the floor, he ran to his mother and clung to her, crying.

'It is a cellar,' Jack told Brad. He held out an oil lantern he had brought from below. 'Here, see if you can light this.'

Brad took a match out of his pocket and lit the wick. The flame sputtered at first, then caught and burned steadily. Brad passed the lantern back to Jack. 'Is there anything else down there?'

Jack nodded and climbed back down the rickety wooden ladder. Brad lowered himself on to the ladder and descended to the cellar. The air smelled old, musty. The room had been dug in the earth and the walls were cold and wet. The space was small and Brad had to bend over to avoid scraping his head on the floorboards above.

'Looks like whoever built this cabin was a prospector,' Jack said, shining the lantern over a collection of digging implements piled in one corner. The rust of time had attacked the shovels and pickaxes and turned them into useless hunks of flaky metal. A small table had once stood near the digging things but had long since gone rotten and collapsed. A scattering of rolled-up papers lay on the floor. Brad picked one up and unrolled it.

Jack held the lantern closer. 'Looks like a map of the area,' he said. His eyes wandered over the spidery diagram then he grabbed the paper and studied it closer. 'Oh my God,' he whispered. 'Black River.'

'What?' Brad asked.

Jack seemed intent on the map. His

brown eyes were wide and a look of worry had crept into his face. He turned to the ladder and started climbing it, taking the map with him. Brad followed him, trying to control an anger which threatened to grow within him. Yet again, Jack was acting mysteriously. Well, this time, Brad was determined to get some straight answers.

Jack laid the map out in front of the fire and extinguished the oil lamp. It was getting dark outside but the fire threw enough light around the cabin for everyone to see the scrawl on the map. Jack pored over it, shaking his head slowly.

Kate and Patrick came over to see what had attracted the black man's interest and Brad joined them, kneeling next to Kate. 'How's Patrick?' he asked her.

'He's OK,' she replied. 'Just a little shaken.'

'I don't believe it,' Jack said, still staring at the map. 'Black River. I knew he was heading for somewhere.

I knew he had a purpose.'

'Who?' Patrick asked, moving next to Jack. 'Did I do good finding the cellar?'

Jack nodded. 'Yeah,' he said. 'Real good.'

The boy grinned widely.

'Black River,' Jack said, looking at Brad. 'I didn't know it was so close. Dyer's heading for Black River.'

'Never heard of it,' Brad replied.

'It's a small town tucked into the other side of those mountains to the west.' He grinned. 'We can stop him if we can cross the mountains by a shorter route. We can get there ahead of him.'

'How do you know he's headed for that town? There must be a dozen towns in that area.'

Jack shook his head. 'He's headed for Black River.'

'What makes you so sure?' Brad asked. Before Jack could answer, he quickly added, 'I want a straight answer this time, Jack. No more half-answers.'

'All right,' Jack said simply. 'Dyer's heading for Black River because there's someone there he thought was dead, until recently.'

'Who?'

Jack left the map and walked to the window. He watched the snow hit the glass and slide down it, leaving wet streaks like tears. 'A lady named Avril Dyer,' he said.

'Avril *Dyer*? Who is she, his wife? Sister?'

Jack continued to watch the snow outside. 'No,' he said. 'Avril Dyer is John Dyer's mother.'

'His mother?' Brad thought for a moment. 'You said he thought she was dead until recently?'

Jack nodded.

'How could he think his mother was dead if she wasn't?' Kate cut in.

'That's what she wanted him to think,' Jack replied. 'It's a long, complex story.'

'Well,' Brad said, 'we've got time to hear it. We won't be going anywhere until morning and I want to know about this man we're chasing. And I want some questions answering, Jack. You know a hell of a lot more than you're telling us.'

Jack watched the raging storm and sighed. 'All right, Brad. I guess I do owe you an explanation.' He pointed to his head. 'Dyer,' he said slowly, 'isn't right up here. He doesn't see the world like we do. His mind twists things around.'

'Are you saying he's crazy?' Brad asked.

Jack turned back to the window and Brad could see that telling this story was painful for him. He remembered Jack's remark at the river about not having a brother any more and he knew that the black man wasn't only here because he had been hired by Dyer's father; Jack was on a *personal* mission of vengeance. The pain lining his face betrayed that fact.

'Dyer isn't crazy,' Jack said. 'Not in the sense you mean. He's ill. A long time ago, some bad things happened to him and he never got over them.'

'What things?' Brad asked. He wanted to know every detail of Dyer's past because he knew that Jack and his brother fitted in there somewhere. He supposed his job as sheriff had taught his mind to try to sort out all the facts, to dispel all mystery. His curiosity had to be satisfied.

'Some things to do with his mother, Avril,' Jack replied. 'Which is why we have to find her before he does.'

'What do you mean?'

'He wants to kill her,' Jack said flatly.

Kate gasped. 'But why would he want to . . . do that?'

'I told you he doesn't see things like we do. Because of what happened in his past, and now that he knows his mother is alive and living in Black River, Dyer is heading there to kill her. He . . . ' Jack stopped and peered out of the window, his gaze suddenly intent. He pushed himself away from the window and sprawled on the floor as shots sounded from outside and a hail of bullets shattered the glass. Kate and Patrick screamed. Brad pulled his gun and pushed the two to the floor, lying down himself as the firing continued and shards of glass skittered over the floor.

'It's Dyer and Henry Ward,' Jack shouted over the noise. His Peacemaker was in his hand and he was loading it with the bullets from his pants pocket. Brad reloaded his own gun.

The shooting stopped and the only sound was the whispering wind. Flakes of snow found their way in through the shattered window and floated to the floor, melting among the shards of glass there.

Brad crawled toward the wall, carefully avoiding the broken glass littering the floor, and stood up next to the window. He risked a quick glance toward the trees but he couldn't see anyone out there. Dyer and Ward had hidden themselves well. Brad slipped back down to the floor and crawled toward Jack.

'Any ideas?' he asked the black marshal.

Jack looked around the cabin then shook his head. 'We're trapped,' he said. 'There's only the one door and if we try to leave by it, we'll be exposed, easy targets.'

'So we've got to take out Dyer and Ward.'

Jack nodded in agreement.

'They're hidden in the trees,' Brad said. 'I can't see them out there.'

'Maybe we can hold them off,' Jack suggested.

'For a while,' Brad agreed. 'But it's getting dark. As soon as night falls, they could sneak up to the door and we'd never see them.' He looked at Kate and Patrick. She looked terrified and her son was trembling as she held him tightly. As he saw the fear in their eyes, Brad felt an emotion sweep through him. He didn't analyse that emotion, though; now was not the time for such things.

A raucous laugh came from outside the cabin. Brad and Jack moved to the window, guns ready. A voice came on the wind. 'This'll teach you to follow us, mister.'

'It's Henry Ward,' Jack whispered to Brad.

Brad looked at Kate and Patrick again and again he felt a flood of emotion for them. 'Jack,' he said, 'maybe you can talk us out of this. Maybe if you talk to Dyer . . . '

'No,' Jack interrupted. 'If Dyer realizes it's me who's on his trail, I don't know how he'll react.'

Brad looked at Kate and Patrick. 'But it's worth a try. He's got us trapped in here. If you talk to him it can't get any worse.'

Jack considered for a moment then nodded. Staying well away from the shattered window, he shouted, 'John, there's a woman and child in here.'

Ward laughed again. 'You hear that, John? The son of a bitch is trying to talk his way out.' Brad tried to locate the sound of the voice but the wind made it impossible.

Another voice came from the trees. But unlike Ward's brash voice, this one sounded nervous, scared almost. 'Who is that in there?'

Jack shouted back, 'You know who I am, John.'

'No.' Dyer's voice sounded faint. The wind almost drowned it out. 'No, I don't know who you are.' He sounded as if he was trying to convince himself.

'Yes you do,' Jack replied. 'It's Jack.'

'Jack who?' Dyer sounded more frightened now. His voice trembled so much, Brad could almost imagine Dyer out there in the trees shaking with fear. Still, he didn't know why. Jack had told him he could beat Dyer and it seemed that Dyer believed it as well.

'You know who I am,' Jack shouted through the remains of the window. 'Deep down, you know it's me who's been following you.'

'Jack who?' Dyer repeated.

'Jack *Hart*,' Jack shouted, emphasizing his surname.

From somewhere among the trees, Dyer suddenly shouted, 'Nooooo!' and a maelstrom of bullets thudded into the wall of the cabin. Jack and Brad dived to the floor and Jack said, 'You were wrong; I think it just got worse.'

★ ★ ★

*Jack Hart*. Hearing that name confirmed Dyer's worst fears. He had to admit that somewhere deep inside himself, he had known it was Jack Hart trailing him. But the confirmation, the sound of Jack's voice after all these years, sent panic sweeping through Dyer's mind and body. He emptied his gun in the direction of the cabin and continued pulling the trigger even after there were no rounds left in the barrel and the hammer clicked emptily and steadily on to the empty chambers like a ticking clock.

'John, your gun's empty.' It was

Henry Ward approaching him. Dyer continued to stare at the cabin and at its broken window. He released the cylinder of his gun and let the spent shell casings tumble to the snowy ground. He reloaded the weapon automatically, his eyes fixed to the cabin.

'It's Jack Hart,' he told Ward.

'Yeah.' Ward looked anxious. 'I heard.'

'It's *him*,' Dyer repeated softly.

'The feller you told us about,' Ward said. 'The black feller whose hand you shot up.'

Dyer nodded, only half-listening. His mind was spinning. An image played over his brain: he was standing facing Hart, ready to draw. How many years ago? He couldn't remember. 'He could always beat me,' he said.

'But you got his hand,' Ward reminded him. 'You beat *him*.'

Dyer shook his head slowly. 'That time was different.' He looked at Ward and closed the memories out his mind.

It was easy; the images were jumbled and incoherent anyway. He knew there was something else connected to those memories; something he must not allow himself to remember. He knew that if he saw Jack Hart, if he stood face to face with the man, that memory would return. He couldn't allow that. 'We've got to kill him,' he told Ward.

Ward nodded and reloaded his rifle.

'No,' Dyer said. 'I've got a better idea.' He looked around the woods. 'This time I'm going to make sure he doesn't have a chance.'

He holstered his gun and nodded slowly, grinning. 'It's time to finish a job I started a long time ago.' He looked back at the cabin. 'And this time I'm going to make sure that bastard stays dead.'

# 10

'It's quiet out there,' Brad whispered to Jack. An eerie stillness had descended over the woods around the cabin and Brad found it unnerving.

'Too quiet,' Jack replied. 'I don't like it.' He picked up his shirt and put it on.

'Have the bad men gone away?' Patrick asked hopefully.

'No,' Brad said, peering out of the broken window. 'They're out there somewhere.'

The boy whimpered softly and Kate hugged him tightly.

'Don't worry,' Jack said, winking at Patrick. 'They're no match for Brad and me.'

Patrick wiped his eyes and smiled at Jack.

'You have a way with kids,' Brad said, as the black man crouched next to him near the window. He felt the pang of jealousy returning but wasn't sure why he wanted to impress Patrick. He wondered if he was trying to impress Kate by bonding with her son. He dismissed the thought as ridiculous. He hardly knew the woman. Still, when he saw her, he felt some emotion rising within himself. Kate had had more effect on him in a short time than any of the girls in Bull's Creek had had on him in seven years.

Jack shrugged. 'You just have to know how kids think. They need reassurance that everything is OK.'

'Everything is not OK,' Brad whispered. 'There are two men out there who are trying to kill us.'

'I know,' Jack said watching the snowy trees. 'It's still too quiet. They're up to something out there.'

'So things are *not* OK.'

'No, they're not, but you don't tell a kid that. You don't know much about children, do you?'

Brad shook his head. 'Never had

any.' The statement reminded him of the years he had spent in Bull's Creek; fruitless years during which he had just seemed to be marking time. Even though he was in a dangerous position, trapped in the cabin with two dangerous killers gunning for him, he felt more alive now than he had in the past seven years. It felt good to feel the adrenalin pumping through his body, keying him up for the danger ahead.

'I had a child,' Jack offered.

'You married?' Brad asked. Somehow, he had always thought of Jack as being single, a loner like himself. The muscular black man with the Colt Peacemaker gripped in his one good hand as he peered through the cabin window did not look like a family man. He looked like a gunman, a killer, a hunter. Not a father. But Brad realized there were many hidden depths to this man's character.

'My wife's name is Norma,' Jack said. 'We've been married eight years now. We both love kids so we were over the moon when Michael came along.'

'Michael is your son?' Kate asked. She had been listening to the conversation while Patrick dozed in her arms.

'He was, ma'am, he was,' Jack said softly. A sadness spread over his broad face. 'When he was five, Michael died of tuberculosis. Norma and me, we looked after him right up to the end. God, we loved him. When he died, it hit us hard. Maybe too hard because now Norma won't have any more children. She's too afraid of losing them like we lost Michael. She doesn't want to go through that pain again. Maybe I don't either because when she told me we wouldn't be having any more kids, I didn't argue. I just accepted it. Maybe we're *both* afraid.'

'I think you'd make a good father,' Kate offered. 'If you had another child, the chances of the same thing happening . . . '

'I know,' Jack said softly. 'But when

something like that happens, it's so bad, you'll do anything to avoid it happening to you again.'

Kate frowned. 'Even if it means giving up on something you've always wanted?'

'Maybe,' Jack said. 'Norma and I are happy together. We visit Michael's grave together and talk about the good times we had with him. We've got a small farm in Colorado.'

'But you came all this way west to find Dyer,' Brad said. He knew he was probing into an area Jack didn't like to talk about but his lawman's curiosity kept niggling at him, pushing him to find Jack's real reason for undertaking this manhunt.

Jack nodded. 'Finding Dyer is something I have to do. I have to stop him.'

'Jack,' Brad said, 'if I ask you a question will you answer it honestly and in a straight manner?'

'I always do that,' Jack answered, and Brad noticed a trace of a smile play over the black man's lips.

'It's just that I'm a naturally curious man,' Brad said. 'My mind likes to have all the facts straight. It's just my way, I guess.'

'OK,' Jack said. 'I'll answer your question.'

'Well,' Brad said, not sure how to begin. His question was delicate and he didn't want to upset Jack. His relationship with the man had turned into a sort of friendship and Brad didn't want to destroy that by asking a question that would make Jack think Brad had been absorbing facts about him, making connections. 'I'm here, on Dyer's trail, because he was responsible for my mother's death,' he continued. 'I know you're not here just because Dyer shot up your hand a long time ago. You wouldn't wait this long to take revenge for that, especially seeing as how you had to leave your wife behind while you came out here to hunt Dyer. Something you said down by the river made me think that maybe you're here for another reason.'

He hesitated. Jack watched him silently, offering nothing.

Finally, after a moment's consideration, Brad voiced his opinion. 'Are you after Dyer because he killed your brother?'

Jack looked out of the window, his eyes roaming the snow-filled sky. When he looked back at Brad, the sadness had returned to his face. 'Yes,' he said. 'John Dyer killed my brother.'

Kate gasped slightly and tears welled up in her eyes. Brad knew why; when you looked at Jack Hart, a gentle and kind man, and realized that death had punctured his life by taking his brother and his son, yet here he was, helping others and trying his damned best to prevent more killing, your heart went out to him. You felt that this man had been dealt a bad hand all his life. But the fact that he didn't seem bitter about it, that he carried on doing his best, made you feel his losses as if they were your own.

'I'm sorry,' Brad said. 'I didn't mean to pry.'

'It's all right,' Jack replied. 'It would have come out sooner or later.' But the sadness remained on his face and Brad wished he could take the question back. He cursed his heavy-handed curiosity. He still had other unanswered questions about Jack, especially regarding the black man's assertion in Bull's Creek that he had beat Dyer at least a hundred times before, but he pushed those questions to the back of his mind. He had no desire to ask anything more of Jack. Because every question he asked had only one answer: death. He would rather Jack remain mysterious than be forced to reveal any more of his wretched past.

Patrick awoke and wiped the sleep from his eyes. 'What's cooking, Mummy?'

'Nothing,' Kate said, smoothing down the boy's hair. 'You're just dreaming, honey.'

Brad sniffed the air. 'No he's not,'

he said. 'I can smell something too.'
The cloying smell of burning wood had
invaded the cabin.

'Smoke!' Jack shouted, pointing to
the rear wall where white smoke drifted
between the logs and reached into the
room with its curling tendrils.

Brad glanced around, panicking.
Smoke also drifted in from the side
walls. 'He's trying to burn us out!' he
shouted. 'We've got to get out!'

'No,' Jack said, laying a hand on his
arm. 'They'll be covering the door with
their guns.'

'We're trapped,' Brad said. 'We can't
get out but if we stay, we'll be burned
alive.' Flames licked around the log
walls, the wood crackling and popping.
The temperature in the cabin began to
soar and Brad felt sweat trickling down
his back. He moved to the window and
squinted into the gloom. Evening had
fallen and dark shadows obscured the
areas between the trees.

'They're too well hidden,' he told
Jack. 'We don't have a chance of

outgunning them.'

Jack was looking around the room frantically. Patrick was crying and Kate's eyes held a look of desperation.

'Maybe if I can get out there,' Jack said. 'Make a dash for the cover of the trees.'

'Don't be crazy,' Brad told him. 'You won't make it out the door.' He wiped the sweat from his brow. The air seemed to burn his throat as he breathed it in and he knew it would get hotter still soon.

'I've got to try,' Jack said, bounding for the door. He wrenched it open then dived backwards to the floor as a hail of bullets blew the doorway to splinters. Jack got up and brushed himself down. 'We can't go that way.'

'We're stuck,' Kate said. She seemed to Brad to be a strong woman but her voice trembled with dread.

The flames fed on the logs quickly, spreading rapidly up the walls to the cabin roof. The heat in the room became searing and the smoke thickened, threatening to choke the people within. They huddled together in the centre of the floor, away from the burning walls.

Brad put an arm around Kate to comfort her but he felt frustratingly useless. He could offer no words of encouragement. He could do nothing. They were trapped. Kate offered him a frightened smile which looked more like a grimace.

Jack put an arm around Patrick. The boy stared at the walls, mesmerized by the patterns in the bright flames. The map which Jack had laid out on the floor began to curl at the edges as the heat stole the moisture from the paper.

*The map!* Brad started, an idea forming in his mind. 'We've got a chance!' he shouted. He grabbed his saddle and one of the blankets. 'Jack,' he said, 'get your saddle and the other blankets. Quickly! We don't have much time.'

John Dyer watched the flames consume the cabin and grinned widely. The walls of the structure collapsed inwards, flames and sparks leaping up into the winter air. Henry Ward walked through the trees toward the burning pile of logs, rifle in hand. He turned to Dyer.

'Looks like the last of him.'

Dyer nodded. This time, Jack Hart had to be dead. He giggled softly to himself. By killing Jack, he had killed any chance of the memory surrounding Jack's brother returning. That pleased him because the memory was bad. Very bad.

'What are we gonna do with their horses?' Ward asked. He had untied the animals before they had set the cabin alight.

'Set them free,' Dyer said. 'They'll wander along the trail until someone finds 'em. We don't have the time to take them with us; they'll slow us down. We have to get to . . . '

'Black River,' Ward finished.

'Yes, Black River.' Dyer had lost track of the conversation because an unbidden memory had appeared in his mind. A name.

Richard.

He frowned, thinking hard. He knew the name was supposed to mean something. Hadn't Jack Hart's brother been called Richard? Richard Hart?

*No!* his mind screamed at him. He left that trail of thought; he didn't like what lay at the end of it.

'Let's saddle up and get out of here,' he told Ward.

They walked to their mounts and Dyer glanced back at the blazing remains of the log cabin. He grinned again. He enjoyed destroying things.

And destroying Jack Hart was something Dyer had longed to do for so many years. Now Jack was dead, Dyer could relax, almost all reminders of the past eradicated.

Almost.

There was one reminder left in Black

River. And when Dyer found her, he would destroy her too. Laughing softly, he swung on to his saddle and gigged his horse through the woods as the stormclouds above swept apart and the night sky cleared.

# 11

As the cabin burned and logs crashed down above them, Kate, Patrick, Jack and Brad huddled beneath their blankets in the cellar. It had been Brad's idea and Kate had at first thought it to be a crazy one. As they had rushed down the ladder to the dark space dug out of the earth beneath the floorboards, she had felt trapped, enclosed. But as they had lain on the floor, covering themselves with the blankets in an attempt to protect themselves from the smoke which crept below the floor, searching for them, she had seen the sense of coming down here.

It was cooler for one thing. The heat from the inferno above seeped down to them but the walls of the cellar were dug in the cold earth and the heat dissipated before it reached them. The smoke did manage to creep beneath the blanket Kate held over herself and Patrick. It clogged her lungs and she tried to cough it out but every breath refilled her with more of the stuff. Patrick seemed racked with a coughing fit and he writhed on the earthen floor of the cellar, a young boy with the hacking cough of an old man.

'We can't stay here long,' Kate shouted. 'The smoke . . . '

'I know,' Brad shouted back from beneath his blanket. He coughed harshly then continued, 'And the air won't last long down here. The fire will suck it up.'

Kate felt herself begin to panic. She wanted to scream at Brad; his plan had saved them from the fire but now they would suffocate in this dark cellar. She forced herself to remain calm. At least we're alive, she reminded herself.

Above them, the cabin crashed inwards. Kate flinched, afraid that the floor boards would break and the burning logs would spill into the cellar, crushing them all. But the floor held.

For now. Kate could hear the boards creaking and groaning beneath the weight of the burning logs. She could also feel the temperature rising now that the fire raged just above their heads. The blanket felt hot, sticky. Sweat began to pour off her. She felt as if she would suffocate in the heat. 'We've got to get out of here,' she moaned, the panic rising within her.

The crackling of the flames above seemed to taunt them. There was no escape.

Brad coughed again then said, 'I'm sorry. I thought we'd be safe down here. It was a bad idea.'

'We're not dead yet,' Jack said. 'As long as we're alive, we've got a chance.'

Jack's attitude reminded Kate that she had always been a survivor. Whenever she had needed it, she had managed to find an inner strength. She had come here with Joe, to this strange country, and she had changed. She had become stronger. And she had become stronger because she had always been a fighter, refusing to give up in the face of overwhelming odds.

She threw the blanket off her and looked around the smoky cellar. There had to be a way out. The darkness had disappeared to be replaced by an eerie orange glow from the fire above.

The floorboards creaked loudly above her. The smoke tasted bitter in her throat and stung her eyes but she continued her search for some means of escape from this hot, nauseous tomb. The heat and smoke attacked her, trying to drain her of her will and strength but she did what she had done her whole life: she fought back and looked for a way to overcome them. She was a survivor. She had always fought and survived and she determined to do so now.

Her stinging eyes fell upon the rusty digging tools piled in the corner of the cellar. She shook the blanketed figures next to her. 'Brad, Jack, we can get out. We can dig our way out!'

The two men threw off their blankets and followed Kate's pointing finger to the old pickaxes and shovels. 'I don't know,' Brad said. He looked at the earth walls. 'I'm not sure those tools will dig through this earth.'

'We've got to try,' Jack said as he moved to the pile of rusting metal. He hefted a shovel and moved to the wall. He laid a hand on the earth. 'This wall is nearest to the back of the cabin.' He coughed as a heavy cloud of grey smoke descended from above. Swinging the shovel at the cellar wall, he dug the rusting spade into the earth and levered the handle to dislodge the dirt.

The handle snapped.

Jack sprawled on the floor, cursing.

Kate began searching through the pile of old tools. 'There must be something here we can use,' she muttered. The idea of digging their way out had given her hope. She didn't want to lose it now. She found a dirty pickaxe and passed it to Brad. 'Try this.'

Brad swung the axe at the dirt and a clod of earth fell from the wall. He swung again and increased the size of the hole, sweat covering him from the heat and his exertion. Jack grabbed a pickaxe and joined him, timing his swings to hit the dirt as Brad pulled his own axe back. They began to build up a rhythm and soon a pile of dirt covered their boots.

'It's getting hotter,' Kate said, wiping her brow. She looked at the floorboards above. She was sure they must be burning by now. Brad and Jack pulled off their shirts as they dug, sweat glistening on their straining muscles. Brad's Raven amulet swung from his neck, glinting in the orange glow which bathed the cellar. They had managed to scrape a sizeable hole in the soil but the exertion, coupled with the heat and smoke, was taking its toll on the men. Both looked exhausted and the digging had slowed as their muscles tired.

Kate looked at Patrick and her heart lurched, gripped by a sudden panic.

Her son lay still, his eyes closed.

Kate rushed over to him and shook him. 'Patrick!' He lolled around in her arms like a rag doll. Kate felt tears spring to her eyes and run down her cheeks. She softly laid Patrick on the floor and put her ear to his chest. He's still breathing, thank God! She needed to get him out of here. He needed to breathe fresh air. Brad and Jack were still digging, but they were going so slow!

The floorboards at the far end of the cellar gave way with a final *crack* and collapsed into the cellar. Kate screamed. A flaming log crashed down. As it landed, it showered the room with hot sparks.

'Put the fire out!' Jack shouted as he swung his pickaxe at the hole in the wall.

Kate grabbed a blanket from the floor and beat it at the flames. Above, she could see more logs burning through the hole in the floor. It wouldn't be long before they came crashing down, crushing anything beneath them. 'Hurry up with the digging!' she shouted at Brad and Jack.

They had dug a hole big enough to crawl through. Their pickaxes disappeared into it as they dug and Kate guessed the small tunnel to be four feet deep. Their progress was too slow. They would never dig their way out of this earthen tomb before the rest of the logs came down. No chance.

Kate refused to believe that. As Jack had said, as long as they were alive there was always a chance.

The floorboards creaked loudly.

'We're not gonna make it,' Brad said as he dug.

'Keep going,' Jack urged. 'We've got to do it.' But even as he spoke, he slowed his swings of the pickaxe, gasping and choking as the bitter smoke overtook him.

Frantically, Kate rushed to the pile of digging tools. They had to dig faster. Patrick needed fresh air. The thought of her son lying unconscious on the floor sent a surge of strength through her and she pulled at the tangle of metal tools, gripping a shovel. She stopped suddenly, her eyes falling on a wooden box behind the rusty metal implements. Dropping the shovel she had picked up, she looked at the box closely, wiping the dust from its lid to reveal a single word etched into the wood. Her hope, which had become subdued, rose again.

'Brad! Jack!' she called excitedly, dragging the box over to them, 'We can get out. We can do it!'

# 12

Jack held the stick of dynamite with shaking hands. He had exerted too much energy on the digging. He could hardly breathe. His eyes stung. His muscles were exhausted, shaking uncontrollably. 'This dynamite is old,' he said. 'We don't know what'll happen if we light it. Or even if it'll light at all.'

'But we've got to try,' Kate said almost pleadingly.

Jack looked at the hole he and Brad had dug; too small for even one of them to crawl into. He looked at the burning floorboards above them and at Patrick lying on the floor. 'Yeah,' he said. 'We've got to try.' He crouched down and peered into the small hole. 'If we put a few sticks in here, it should be enough to blow a hole through the dirt.'

Brad nodded. 'So let's do it.'

'But,' Jack said. 'the blast will also come back into the cellar. Even if it doesn't injure us, it'll cause a sudden vibration. Those logs above us are balanced at the moment. In the aftershock, they'll come down on top of us.'

'If we don't try it,' Kate said, 'they'll come down on us anyway eventually.' Her eyes were frightened, frantic.

Jack nodded. 'We've got to direct the blast outwards, into the earth.'

'The table!' Brad shouted, pointing to the overturned table in the corner. 'We can set it over the hole, shore it up with some of this earth we dug out.'

'We won't have time to do that before the sticks go off,' Jack said, shaking his head.

'Yes we will,' Brad said. 'We can lengthen the fuse by tying on the fuses from the sticks we don't use.'

Jack looked in the box. There were about a dozen sticks in there. He didn't know much about dynamite but he did know they wouldn't need more than six sticks for what they had in mind. They could use the fuses from the other six to give them time to shore up the hole. It sounded like a slim chance but it was the only chance they had. 'All right,' he said. 'Kate, start tying the fuses together. I think we'll need about six sticks.'

'I haven't seen this stuff used much,' Brad said, 'but I've never seen six sticks used at once. How do you know it isn't too much?'

'I don't.'

'We could end up blowing ourselves up,' Brad pointed out.

'I know,' Jack said. 'But we have to make sure the blast is strong enough to blow an escape hole. That ground is frozen near the surface.' He had no idea how strong a blast six sticks of dynamite would produce. It could be too much and blow the cellar to pieces or it could be too little and leave them trapped.

Brad dragged the broken table near

the hole and found two shovels in the pile of tools. 'Any idea how much time we'll have to set the table in place?' he asked Jack.

'No idea,' Jack replied truthfully. Kate handed him the six sticks of explosive. The newly fashioned fuse was four feet long. 'Move the rest of the sticks well away from the hole,' Jack told her. 'We can't risk them going off.'

He walked to the small tunnel and gingerly set the sticks inside, pulling the fuse so that it reached the edge of the hole. 'As soon as I light it,' he told Brad, 'get the table in place. We'll shore it up as quickly as we can then get under the blankets at the far end of the room. They won't protect us much but they're all we've got.'

A board overhead splintered and a flaming log crashed to the floor. Kate started for it to put out the flames. 'No,' Jack said. 'There's no time.' He lit the fuse and stepped back, helping Brad drag the table over the hole.

They began piling the earth they had deposited on the floor against the table, securing it in place. Jack could hear the fuse hissing in the tunnel, like a snake waiting to strike. He felt himself start to panic. He and Brad had to be across the room when the explosive blew. He had no idea when that would be. They piled as much earth as they dared against the table before Jack dragged Brad across the room. 'Come on,' he said. 'That's enough.'

'Are you sure?' Brad asked as they buried themselves beneath the blankets at the far wall.

'I don't know,' Jack admitted. He waited in the dark beneath the blanket, his muscles strained, ready for the explosion. He couldn't hear the fuse hissing any longer, wouldn't know when it had stopped and was ready to strike.

He heard Kate crying softly. He heard Brad breathing heavily. He heard his own heartbeat, loud and scared.

The explosion, when it finally came,

was deafening. Jack felt as if his ears had burst. Reflexively he put his hands over them but it was too late; they were ringing loudly in his head. All other sounds seemed muffled. Only the ringing was clear. He felt something slam into his side and knock the wind out of him. He realized it was the table. It had shot across the room like a cork popping out of a bottle. He grimaced as he felt his ribs. He was sure something was cracked or broken. Painfully, he pulled the blanket off him and stood up, pushing the table out of the way.

'Is everyone OK?' It hurt him to speak. The table had definitely broken something.

Brad and Kate threw off their blankets and nodded. Jack looked at the tunnel. He had expected to see daylight streaming in but he reminded himself that night had been approaching when they had climbed down into the cellar. He walked painfully across the room and pushed his head into the hole.

He smelled clean, fresh air.

'We've done it,' he said as he pulled his head back. He winced as pain shot through his left side.

Brad clambered into the hole and disappeared into the darkness. 'I'm outside!' he shouted back to them. He climbed back through and took Patrick from Kate. He held the boy tightly and clambered back through the tunnel.

'You next,' Jack told Kate.

She nodded and crawled into the tunnel. Jack waited until her feet disappeared into the darkness then dragged his and Brad's saddles to the mouth of the dark tunnel. He heaved his saddle into the hole and clambered in after it, dragging Brad's saddle behind him. Pain lanced through him as he squeezed through the hole, pushing and pulling the heavy leather saddles. He could not leave them behind; he and Brad would need their rifles and equipment.

The darkness in the earthen tunnel seemed to cling to him, then he felt himself surrounded by a different darkness, the darkness of the night. He was outside. He realized he had been holding his breath in the tunnel and he let it out now and breathed in the fresh, clean air of the night. Standing painfully, he stared at the stars shining in the dark sky.

'Storm's passed over,' he observed.

Patrick was on the ground, coughing now that his lungs had tasted the crisp night air. Kate was kneeling over him, shedding quiet tears of relief. Brad knelt next to her, his arms around her.

Jack could imagine how relieved Kate must feel to see Patrick recovering. He thought of his own son, Michael. He and Norma had never been able to cry tears of relief, only of sorrow. His mind turned to a more recent memory: his own father crying tears of frustration over what had happened to Richard. Jack had ridden to his father's house and found the man in tears on the back porch, sitting in his creaky old rocking chair and just staring at the woods while tears ran down his cheeks.

'What's wrong, Pa?' he had asked, already knowing the answer to the question.

'Just thinking about Richard,' John Hart had replied, still staring at the trees and rocking back and forth in the chair.

'And Dyer?'

His father had nodded slowly. 'Of course. I can't seem to remember Richard any more without thinking about Dyer too. I try to tell myself to forget about him, just think of the good times, but somehow it always ends with Dyer. I'll never get the events of that day out of my mind for as long as I live.'

Jack nodded and sat on the porch while his pa got control of his tears.

'How's your hand, Son?'

'Still hurts sometimes,' Jack replied. 'Sometimes, I can even feel the fingers itching. I go to scratch them before I remember they aren't there any more.'

'I guess you'll never forget that day

either,' John Hart said. 'Every time you try to scratch those missing fingers, it'll all come back.'

'I can't forget,' Jack replied. 'But it's not because of my hand. I think about Richard every day and like you, I can't think about him without thinking about Dyer. And when I think about Dyer, I remember that day.'

His father had nodded and continued staring at the woods in silence.

Jack looked at the ruined, burning cabin as Patrick woke up slowly. Thinking of his father had upset him. His pa was a good man and didn't deserve what had happened to his family. But then Norma and I didn't deserve what happened to Michael, he thought. After Michael's death, Jack and his father had become closer. They had both shared a tragedy; each had lost a son.

The burning logs shifted and dropped into the cellar as their structure collapsed. Sparks rose into the night air like bright orange fireflies.

He heard Patrick mumble something behind him and turned to see the boy getting shakily to his feet. He grabbed his mother's hand and she hugged him.

'We'd better get moving,' Jack said. 'We can't stay out here all night.'

Brad nodded then scanned the trees nearby. 'The horses are gone.'

'How far is it to your farm, Kate?'

'About a mile and a half.'

'We'll walk,' Jack said.

'I don't think Patrick can make it that far,' she replied.

'I can carry him,' Jack offered. But as soon as he said the words, he knew he could not carry the boy; his entire left side felt as if it were on fire. It hurt him to breathe.

'I'll do it,' Brad said, as if reading Jack's thoughts. He bent down in front of the boy. 'Would you like to go for a ride?' he asked.

Patrick nodded weakly.

'OK, climb on my back and hang on tight,' Brad said. Patrick clambered on to his back and wound his arms around Brad's neck. Brad stood up and said, 'OK, let's go.'

They set off into the trees, Jack dragging the saddles, trudging through the deep snow while behind him the cabin continued blazing angrily. The snow slowed them down and Jack felt frustrated at their sluggish progress. Dyer would be on his way to Black River now and unless Jack got there before him, someone else would die at the hands of the outlaw.

And Jack was determined not to let that happen.

# 13

They found the horses half a mile along the trail. The animals had stayed together and wandered into the trees. After they had saddled Jack's stallion and Brad's pinto and tethered Kate's horses to their saddles, they mounted up and trotted toward the farmhouse. Brad and Patrick rode the pinto while Jack and Kate led the way on the stallion.

Jack felt more comfortable now that he was in the saddle. The half-mile walk had been agony for him. His ribs felt like they were cutting through his side and the pain had increased with every step. Still, he knew he wouldn't have time to rest even when they reached the farmhouse; he needed to keep moving, to catch up with Dyer again, to stop him. Before it was too late.

He shifted in the saddle and winced as searing pain shot along his left side.

'We're nearly there,' Kate said. 'Does it hurt a lot?'

'I can't remember being in this much pain before. Ever.'

'Not even when . . . ?' She stopped, as if unsure how to finish her question.

'When Dyer shot my fingers off?' he finished for her. He shook his head. 'I was in shock. Didn't feel a thing, really. Besides, most of the nerves in my hand were destroyed, so I couldn't feel the pain.'

'It must have been awful.'

'At the time, yes. I had to relearn everything left-handed. I can't use my right hand for anything except holding light objects. There's no grip there. I couldn't use it to hold a gun, for example. But I can hold the reins to steer my horse. It isn't so bad. It could have been worse.' He stopped as he remembered his brother. 'A lot worse.'

'It must have taken a lot of willpower to get over it, though.'

'I guess so, but we all have problems we have to overcome. I'm sure you had a tough time when your husband died.'

She shrugged. 'He was a lousy husband.'

'But you still must have found it rough, bringing up your son and working the farm on your own.'

'Yes,' she said. 'But I learned to cope eventually and it turned me into a stronger person.'

He nodded. 'We overcome our problems and move on.'

'Or we go back and try to take revenge,' she said slowly.

He grinned and shook his head. 'No,' he said. 'I'm not chasing Dyer to get revenge for this.' He held up his right hand.

'For your brother, then?'

He shook his head.

'So you're doing it just because the US Marshals' office has hired you?'

she asked pointedly. 'The only reason you're here is because Dyer's father wants you to kill his son?'

'It isn't like that at all,' Jack replied.

She was silent for a few moments and Jack looked over at Brad and Patrick riding beside him. Brad was trying to start a conversation with the boy but Patrick was having none of it. He sat silently in the saddle while Brad continued talking.

Jack had noticed at the cabin that Brad had seemed anxious to befriend the boy. He knew why; he had seen the way Brad looked at Kate. Brad probably thought that if Patrick liked him, Kate would grow to like him as well. But what Brad did not know was that children could see through any half-hearted attempts to win their favour. Brad's endeavours were actually counter-productive, making Patrick wary of him and placing a barrier between the two. Brad was trying too hard, not able to relax and be himself.

And the irony, Jack knew, was that

183

Kate was *already* attracted to Brad. He had noticed the look in her eyes when she spoke to him, something which Brad had obviously missed because it was a reflection of what was in his own eyes and he had been blinded to it.

Jack shook his head, smiling to himself.

'So why are you *really* here, Jack?' Kate asked him, picking up the conversation where it had left off.

He considered telling her about Richard Hart, about John Dyer, about his father. But he was tired and in pain. He did not have the energy to tell her everything. And that was what he would have to do to make her understand why he was here, on Dyer's trail. He would not be able to compress the facts into an abridged version. Everything fitted together. All the pieces locked into place with each other, each one dependent on the others. Like a complex puzzle, the pieces fitted together in a pattern of death; a pattern which had sent Jack out to hunt down the man who called himself John Dyer. Hunt down and shoot him.

'It's a long story,' he told Kate, hoping that the finality in his voice would stop her questions.

She simply nodded as if she understood that he didn't want to talk about it and fell silent again.

'We're home!' Patrick shouted excitedly. He was smiling for the first time since he had beaten Jack at the mock gunfight at the cabin, before he had fallen into the cellar.

They rode off the main trail and headed toward the farmhouse, a long, low, stone structure surrounded by barns and outbuildings. 'Welcome to the Donnelley farm,' Kate said, as she slid from the saddle. Jack could see she was glad to be home. He dismounted and gritted his teeth as sharp pain bit into his ribs.

Brad helped Patrick slide down out of the saddle and the boy ran to his mother's side. 'I'll fix us something to eat,' Kate said to Jack and Brad. 'You can take the horses to the barn.' She pointed then headed for the house with Patrick following her.

Jack and Brad led the horses into the barn and found four empty stalls. As Jack removed the saddle from his horse, he watched Brad. The ex-sheriff seemed pensive, troubled.

'You OK?' Jack asked.

Brad looked up from the cinch strap he was untying and nodded. He set to work on the strap again then heaved the saddle off his horse and laid it on the barn floor. He found a set of grooming brushes and returned to the pinto, stroking the brushes over its neck lovingly. Still silent, still brooding.

'Do you want to talk about it?' Jack asked.

Brad shook his head and continued grooming the pinto. Jack started grooming his own horse but still watched Brad. He considered the ex-lawman his friend and didn't like it that he was troubled by something.

'Is it Kate?'

Brad shrugged. 'Maybe. I guess so. I don't know.'

Jack left it at that and patted the stallion's neck. He set his saddle on the floor and started toward the door. 'Time to eat,' he said.

'Jack,' Brad said from behind him, stopping him before he reached the door. Jack turned to face his friend.

Brad hesitated as if unsure how to continue. Then he said, 'When this is all over, what are you going to do?'

'Go back to Norma,' Jack said.

'I suppose you miss her.'

Jack nodded. 'A hell of a lot,' he said truthfully.

Brad sighed. 'After I go to see my sister and father, I'll be drifting again. Right back where I was years ago.'

'You could have stayed in Bull's Creek,' Jack reminded him. 'You had a job and a home.'

Brad shook his head. 'I was never happy there. I always thought there had to be more.'

'And you think helping me stop Dyer will destroy that restlessness?'

Brad shrugged and shook his head. 'No, of course not. But it's gotten me moving again. I feel like I've broken out of a cage, like I've shrugged off shackles that I've worn for so long I didn't even know they were there. But now I'm afraid of slipping back into the old pattern. Drifting again and settling in another Bull's Creek.'

'Why were you unhappy there?' Jack asked.

'I didn't find what I wanted.'

'What is it you want?'

'I guess I always wanted to find a wife, settle down with her and have kids.'

Jack nodded and turned to the door. 'Come on, let's get something to eat.'

They left the barn and walked toward the farmhouse. 'I'm leaving in the morning,' Jack said. 'If you don't want to come, if you want to stay here . . . '

'Of course I'm coming,' Brad said.

'Why would I not want to come?'

Jack looked at the night sky. The stars shone clear and perfect in their geometric patterns. 'I thought maybe you and Kate . . . '

'No,' Brad said simply.

'She likes you, you know,' Jack said.

'What? Has she said something?'

Jack shook his head as they neared the farmhouse door. 'She doesn't have to. Her eyes say it all.'

'Her boy doesn't like me at all,' Brad said.

'Only because you're trying too hard to get him to like you,' Jack replied. 'Don't. Kids can see through it.'

They reached the farmhouse door and entered the kitchen where the mouth-watering smells of bacon, eggs and warm bread assailed them. Kate stood at the stove, piling the food on to plates, while Patrick sat at the kitchen table. Jack sat next to him and winced as the pain in his ribs flared.

'I can go into town in the morning and fetch the doctor,' Kate offered.

'I'm afraid we don't have time,' Jack said. 'We have to be moving in the morning.'

She nodded and placed the plates of food on the table. Jack noticed the disappointment in her face. 'I have some bandages,' she said. 'I'll strap it up for you. It won't help much but it's better than nothing.'

'That'd be fine,' Jack said. 'Kate, would it be all right if Brad and I leave our horses here while we go on to Black River?'

'Won't you be needing them?'

He shook his head. 'If Dyer and Ward have been on the move since they set fire to the cabin, they'll be too far ahead for us to catch up in time. By the time we get to Black River, they will have been and gone. So we're going to go on foot.'

'What are you talking about?' Brad asked, confused.

'Remember the map at the cabin? Black River is just on the other side of the mountains to the west. But the trail winds *around* the mountains. Dyer will be following that trail. But we're going to go straight over the mountains. It's a shorter, more direct route. We'll get to Black River before he does.'

'Over the mountains?' Brad asked, sounding doubtful.

'It won't be easy,' Jack said, 'but it's the only way we can beat Dyer.'

'All right.' Brad nodded and finished his meal. 'That was delicious, Kate.'

She smiled at him.

'Well,' Jack said as he cleared his plate, 'I think it's time we got some sleep. We've got a long day ahead tomorrow.'

★ ★ ★

Kate couldn't sleep. She had tried to relax but her mind was spinning. Patrick had almost died in the cabin. She checked on him constantly throughout the night and found him sleeping soundly, the only sign of his earlier experience a slight wheeze in his breathing. Kate decided it was pointless trying to sleep so she wrapped a shawl around her shoulders and went out to the porch to look at the stars. She often sat outside at night when she needed to think.

She found Brad sitting on the porch steps, smoking and staring out into the night toward the mountains.

'Couldn't sleep?' she asked him.

He looked up at her and shook his head. 'You?'

'No,' she said as she sat beside him on the wooden steps. 'I keep thinking about Patrick. He's been through a lot today.'

Brad nodded and drew on his smoke. 'We all have.' He tossed the cigarette to the ground and it landed with a flourish of bright orange sparks.

'Were you thinking about your mother?' Kate asked him.

'Yeah, I guess so. My whole family, really. It's strange; all those years in Bull's Creek I never really thought about them at all. Then last week I

192

found an old photograph. I decided I was going to go back to Wyoming, to visit them all.' He sighed deeply. 'Now I can't.'

'There's still your father and sister,' Kate said. She couldn't bear to see Brad depressed. After hearing about Jack's brother and son, she had heard enough talk about death. 'I'm sure they'll be glad to see you after all this time.'

'Maybe,' Brad said. 'Laura will, I guess. As for my father, I doubt it. I was never good enough for him.' He lit another smoke and stared at the dark night. 'Never.' He looked at her and smiled. 'Still, after this business with Dyer is over, I'm heading for Wyoming to see them.'

Kate felt her heart sink. Wyoming. A long way. 'Are you going to settle there?' she asked, trying to sound unconcerned.

He looked at her closely and she felt her pulse quicken. She had realized, since their first meeting in the cabin, that Brad Harris was the type of man she had thought Joe was when she had married him. Brad was a man of action; decisive, determined. He was everything Joe could never have been, everything she needed.

'I don't think I'll stay in Wyoming too long,' he said. He shrugged. 'I don't know what I'll do. I can't go drifting around the country forever.'

'If it's work you need,' she said quickly, 'I could use some help on the farm. It's a growing enterprise and I'll need someone who knows something about animals. Do you know much about cattle?'

Brad smiled, then laughed softly, shaking his head slowly.

'What's so funny?' she asked him.

'I'm just thinking about something Jack said to me when we were settling the horses in the stable,' he said. 'I do know a lot about cattle, Kate. I worked on a few ranches in Montana some time ago. But I don't want to come and work for you.'

'Oh,' she said, trying to keep the disappointment out of her voice. She chastised herself for letting herself fall for this man in such a short time.

'But,' Brad said, looking at her, 'after I've visited Laura and my pa, I would very much like to come back here to see you.'

She felt herself grinning at him. He reached out and touched her arm. The touch sent shivers through her. He had touched her before, in the cabin, to comfort her, but this was different. She put her hands on his shoulders and felt the solid muscles beneath his shirt. They leaned closer to each other and kissed.

In the east, the sun forced its way above the horizon slowly, casting an amber glow over the farm, the house and the mountains to the west. Beyond those mountains lay Death, but for now the two figures on the porch basked in the pure light of dawn.

# 14

John Dyer awoke before dawn, the remnants of the nightmare still fresh in his mind. It was the same every night, had been the same for so long now that he would have expected it to lose its frightening power over him. But it tortured him with the same ferocity as it had done for so many years.

*The hands. The hands pulling me down. Can't breathe in the blackness. But they're still holding me, dragging me down into the dark.*

He threw off his blankets and walked to the dying fire. It had been kept alight all night to keep him and Ward from freezing as they slept amongst the cold rocks by the trail. He poked the embers with a stick from the pile they had collected last night and lit a smoke. Throwing the stick on to the flames and watching them consume it, he tried to get the memory of the nightmare out of his head. But, as was usually the case on the worst days, it clung to him.

It was always the same: unseen hands dragging him down into a darkness which seemed to smother him, stealing his breath and taking away his ability to hear or see anything. Until, finally, something would come floating to him through the blackness; faint and pale at first, then, as it got closer, familiar and terrifying.

The face.

*Richard Hart's face.*

Grinning.

Alive.

The sight of the face would wake Dyer, sweating and shaking. The world seemed to spin when he awoke from the nightmare and he would take a few moments to recover from it. For a few minutes, he wouldn't know where he was, who he was. His mind would only focus on one thing: Richard's face. Then, as reality slowly reasserted itself, he would remember that Richard Hart was dead.

*Had* to be dead.

He was now just a memory, a dream. A frightening dream but a dream nonetheless.

Dyer threw the smoke away and it fizzled out in the snow. He had lost his taste for it. He had things to do today; big things. He walked over to where Ward slept amongst the rocks and kicked him.

Ward sat up, wiping the sleep from his eyes. 'Goddammit, John, what time is it?'

'Time to get up.'

Ward crawled from beneath his blankets and staggered to the fire. He sat by the flames, warming himself. The sky brightened as the sun came up in the east and Dyer felt the nightmare losing its grip on him. He grinned. His memories of Richard always faded along with the darkness. Richard had no power over Dyer during the daylight hours because Richard was just a ghost, a dream. He was dead.

Dead. Dyer reminded himself. I killed him a long time ago. That thought brought a question to his mind but he quickly forced it out of his head and started to saddle his horse.

Ward looked at him. 'Ain't we gonna have coffee before we start off?'

Dyer shook his head. 'No time, Henry. I want to take care of business in Black River as quickly as possible.' Maybe then the nightmares will stop, he told himself. Ward sighed and kicked snow over the fire. He saddled up and swung on to his horse.

They set off along the trail at a steady pace. As the sun rose higher and the mountains turned orange with the early morning glow, Dyer breathed in a deep lungful of air and grinned.

Today, he was going to kill the last link with his past.

And he hoped that when he did that, he would also kill the ghost which had haunted him all these years.

Brad had started the climb over the mountains feeling elated. After last night, he felt as if he belonged somewhere now, with Kate. He knew it was too soon and that everything had happened so fast but something about Kate Donnelley felt right. The reticence he had felt when he was with the women in Bull's Creek had disappeared. With Kate, he knew it would work.

He had begun to climb behind Jack feeling alive and strong. Now, though, he felt tired. They had been climbing for hours and Brad could feel every muscle aching and hurting. Because of the cold, they were wrapped in scarves and gloves, which had proved to be fine at first but now made Brad feel suffocated. His body temperature had risen during the climb and he could feel sweat running down his back and sides beneath his heavy coat.

He had slowed considerably during

the last half-hour and now Jack was well ahead of him, clambering over the snowy rocks like a mountain lion. The pain in his side, which Kate had strapped up before they left this morning, seemed to have been forgotten. Now that they were near Black River, Jack seemed to be driven on by some inner strength. Brad felt as if his lungs and throat were on fire as he gasped in cold snatches of air. He would have to stop soon and rest.

He looked up. Jack had reached the top of the rocks and stood looking to the west. When I get there, I can rest, Brad thought. He clambered on, determined to reach Jack. When he finally made it to the top, he wheezed and panted, sitting heavily on the rocks next to his friend.

'Black River,' Jack said, pointing west.

The small town lay in the shadow of the mountains next to a winding, frozen river. 'So this is where it all ends,' Brad said. 'Black River. This is where we kill Dyer.' Looking at the small town, he felt somehow let down. After what he and Jack had been through to get here, he had expected more. But this was where the hunt would end. The trail of death left by Dyer led here; a small insignificant town in the middle of nowhere.

'Listen,' Jack said, 'there's something we have to discuss.'

Brad nodded, willing to discuss anything Jack wanted. The longer they put off the climb down to the town, the longer he had to catch his breath.

'When we find them,' Jack said, 'I want you to take care of Ward; Dyer's mine.'

'All right.' Brad wasn't going to argue. If Dyer was as quick with a gun as Jack seemed to think he was — to *know* he was — then the best person to face him would be Jack. Brad had come along knowing that in the end it would be Jack who killed Dyer. As long as he was part of the hunt and was there when Dyer finally received justice, he would feel satisfied. Then he could go to his father and sister with the news that Edna Harris's death had been avenged.

Then he could return to Kate.

'It's important to you, isn't it,' he said to Jack, 'that you're the one who pulls the trigger?'

Jack looked at him squarely. 'More important than you know, Brad.'

'Well just as long as you don't miss, I'll be happy.'

'I won't miss.' A smile crossed Jack's face and he started down the mountain toward Black River.

Taking a deep breath of chill air, Brad clambered after him.

# 15

Dyer and Ward rode into town from the east, past the sheriff's office and the row of businesses lining the main drag. Dyer could scarcely contain his excitement. He could feel his muscles trembling as adrenalin coursed through them. Yet that excitement was tinged with fear. Fear of seeing his mother.

Seeing her would bring back the memories.

He slid from his saddle and hitched his horse to a post outside the Six Shots Saloon. Ward did likewise and the two men walked through the batwings. Dyer ordered whiskey and slaked the thirst he had picked up on the trail. He looked the bartender in the eye and said, 'Me and my partner here, we're looking for a lady who lives in these parts. Perhaps you'd be so kind as to tell me where we might find her. Avril Dyer.'

The bartender thought for a minute, scratching his head, then nodded. 'Yeah, I know the lady you're talking of. But I just can't go telling no strangers where she is. Wouldn't be right. All I know, you could be anybody.'

Dyer reached across the bar and grabbed the man's shirt, pulling him closer. 'Listen to me,' he said tightly, 'I ain't a stranger to Avril Dyer: I'm her goddamn son.'

The bartender's eyes widened slightly and Dyer saw fear there. 'Avril Dyer didn't have no son.'

Dyer sneered. 'Are you calling me a liar, mister?'

'No,' the bartender said. 'If you say you're her son, that's good enough for me. I just ain't heard of no son, that's all.' He tried to pull back but Dyer held his shirt fast.

'Mister, your wisest course of action right now is to tell me where I can find my mother,' Dyer whispered. He felt himself wanting to kill this man. Killing was the only way to forget.

'All right,' the bartender said softly, as if he were trying to calm Dyer down. 'I'll tell ya where ya can find old Avril. If you ask around long enough, someone'll tell ya anyways, so I don't see how it can hurt. She's on Cedar Street, west end of town.'

'Which house?'

'You'll find her. Only place *on* Cedar Street.'

Dyer released his grip and grinned. He wheeled around and left the saloon with Ward following on his heels. He stopped on the boardwalk and felt a wave of dizziness wash over him. He leaned against the hitching rail and closed his eyes while trying to shake off the nausea. Ward said, 'You all right, John?' His voice sounded distant.

'Yeah,' Dyer said. The world seemed to be spinning. He *wasn't* all right at all.

*The darkness.*

He opened his eyes and looked into the sun but his mind played a scene over and over. The nightmare.

*The hands pulling him down.*

The memories had never come during the day before. This scared him. He staggered across the drag and collided with a couple of townsfolk.

'Watch where you're goin',' he heard someone say but he was lost. Lost to the scenes playing through his mind.

*The face.*

'John!' He felt Ward gripping his shoulders, holding him upright. His legs had lost all their strength.

*Richard Hart's face.*

'No!' He pushed Ward away from him and spun around. He was running. Running west through town. He pulled his gun from its holster. He had to find his mother now. Killing her would stop the dreams. He increased his pace, running wildly through the streets. His lungs felt as if they were bursting. His throat burned. It didn't matter. All that mattered now was finding Avril Dyer. Finding her and killing her.

★ ★ ★

207

Henry Ward struggled to keep up with Dyer. He wasn't even sure if he wanted to keep up. He had never seen John like this before. They had ridden together for a long time and Ward knew that Dyer had moments when he appeared unbalanced, as if he were struggling to hold on to his sanity. But now, he seemed to have lost that struggle. Ward sucked in air and tried to ignore the ache in his legs as he ran after him.

Finally, he had to slow down. He lost sight of Dyer when he sprinted around a row of houses. Ward slowed to a painful walk. He held his aching sides and continued on after John. He knew that the black man they had killed in the cabin had held some of the answers to Dyer's condition. Dyer had spoken of him often and when he had found that it was Jack Hart who was trailing them, he had begun his slide from reality. Now, it seemed he would never return from his descent into madness.

Ward rounded a corner and noticed

the sign for Cedar Street. He increased his pace as much as he could and entered the street, searching for a house. The bartender had said Avril Dyer was in the only house on Cedar Street.

Ward looked around, confused.

There were no houses on Cedar Street.

Only a small, fenced-in cemetery. Ward spotted Dyer behind the fence, kneeling on the ground before a gravestone, head lowered. Then he remembered.

The bartender had said Avril Dyer was in the *only place* on Cedar Street.

Ward walked through the gate in the wrought-iron fence and made his way through the trees and gravestones to where his friend knelt in the dirt. They had come here so that John could kill Avril Dyer. Why, Ward had no idea, but nature had beaten Dyer and had taken Avril before he could find her. Perhaps now, the madness would end.

Dyer seemed to have calmed down. He knelt with his head bowed as if in prayer and Ward noticed tears streaming down his cheeks and falling into the dirt of the grave. He stayed a respectable distance away, deciding to let Dyer choose his own time to speak.

But Dyer seemed aware of his presence and said, 'She's dead.'

Ward frowned. Dyer had come here to kill Avril and now he had found her already dead, he was upset. It made no sense.

'She's dead,' Dyer repeated.

'Yeah,' Ward said, not knowing what else to say.

'She's dead but the dreams still keep coming.'

'Dreams?'

Dyer nodded. standing up. 'The dreams of Richard Hart.'

'The feller you killed a long time ago? Jack Hart's brother?'

Dyer nodded and wiped the tears from his eyes. 'I dream of him every night. And when I do, I know I killed him but I don't know *how* I killed him. It's all confused. Jack Hart knew. So I had to kill him, Henry. I had to. Because whatever happens, I must never remember how I killed Richard Hart.' He pointed to the grave. 'And she knew about Richard too. I had to come here to kill her.'

Ward felt confused. 'But they're both dead now, John. It's all right.'

Dyer shook his head savagely and the tears flew from his cheeks. 'No! It isn't all right! I thought that if they were dead, the nightmare would stop. But it keeps coming to me, Henry. *He* keeps coming to me. And one day, he's going to tell me how I killed him. And I must never know that.'

Ward remained silent. He didn't know what to say or do for his friend. Nothing Dyer said made sense. Yet it seemed to have some meaning to him.

'Perhaps I need to kill some more,' Dyer said half to himself. He looked at Ward. 'Are you afraid to die, Henry?'

Ward felt his gunfighter's instincts scream at him. He saw Dyer's hand edge toward his gunbelt. 'John, what are you doing?'

Dyer was nodding to himself. 'Killing is the only way to forget,' he whispered.

'John, no!'

Dyer's hand paused over the handle of his gun.

Ward panicked. He had seen Dyer's speed and knew he didn't stand a chance if that gun cleared leather. 'John . . . '

Dyer's hand jerked and Ward reached for his own gun, managing to pull it from the holster before Dyer's six-gun exploded and Ward felt hot pain in his chest. He clutched for the wound but his arm seemed to have lost all strength and fell limply to his side. He dropped his gun. He felt his strength being sapped away and the last thing he saw before he died was his friend John Dyer standing over his mother's grave, a smoking gun in his hand.

And behind Dyer, stepping from behind a stand of trees, he saw Jack Hart. He knew Hart was dead and must be a ghost and that the only reason he could see him was because he was now entering the realm of ghosts himself.

★ ★ ★

'John,' Jack said as he stepped out from behind the trees, 'put your gun back in the holster.'

Dyer, facing away from him, stiffened at the sound of Jack's voice. 'You're dead,' he said, frightened. 'I killed you.'

'No,' Jack said. 'Now put that gun back in its holster and turn around. We're going to do this properly.' He glanced at Ward's dead body. So it had become this bad; Dyer had killed his friend. All the more reason he had to be stopped now.

Dyer slid the gun back in its holster but refused to turn around.

'Face me,' Jack said levelly.

'No,' Dyer said, shaking his head.

'We've done this so many times

before, John. Remember the last time? I do. I remember it every time I look at my hand.'

Dyer remained facing away. 'I can't look at you,' he said timidly.

'Because if you look at me, you'll remember won't you, John? You'll remember about Richard Hart. My brother.'

'I killed him,' Dyer said.

'Goddammit, John, face me!'

Dyer turned around slowly, eyes to the ground. When he finally lifted them and saw Jack's face, he gasped and Jack saw understanding flash across his features. Dyer started to cry. 'No, no, no,' he repeated.

'You remember now,' Jack said. 'You remember about Richard Hart.'

Dyer shook his head viciously. 'No! He's dead. I killed him.'

'How did you kill him, John?'

'I don't remember. But I killed him . . .'

Jack shook his head.

'He's dead,' Dyer whimpered.

'Listen to me,' Jack said forcefully. 'You don't remember how you killed him because you *didn't* kill Richard Hart.'

'He's dead,' Dyer repeated. 'He has to be.'

'No, he isn't dead. You know that. You never killed him.'

Dyer started to tremble. He wiped his eyes. They darted around the graveyard, seeming to see everything for the first time. He looked at Jack.

'Jack,' he said. 'I didn't kill him. I tried but I couldn't.' He put his hand to his mouth and began to weep. 'I did bad things, Jack.'

'Yes,' Jack said evenly.

Dyer looked pitiful. He hitched his shoulders as he wept then wiped his eyes with his sleeve. 'I don't think I can stop, Jack.'

'That's why I'm here, John. I've come to stop you.'

Dyer's eyes darted to Jack's Peacemaker. 'To kill me?' He shook his head. 'You can't kill me, Jack.'

'Draw that gun,' Jack said, nodding to Dyer's sidearm.

'I can't beat you, Jack. You know that. You could always beat me. Every time.'

'That was with my right hand,' Jack said. 'I can't hold a gun in that hand any more. I'm using my left now. You have a chance, John.'

Dyer shook his head, watching Jack's left hand. 'I don't think so.'

'No,' Jack conceded, 'neither do I. Because we both know that you want me to win. You want to be stopped.'

Dyer's hand inched toward his gun. His eyes remained fixed on the Peacemaker. Jack flexed the fingers of his left hand and positioned them over his holster.

'Jack,' Dyer said, 'please don't.'

'You have to be stopped,' Jack said.

Tears streamed down Dyer's face. 'I'm afraid to die, Jack.'

Jack said nothing. He waited.

'You can't kill me, Jack; I'm your brother.' He went for the gun then, his right hand becoming a blur of movement.

Jack snapped the Peacemaker from his holster and fired.

★ ★ ★

Brad waited in the trees, watching the exchange between Jack and Dyer. He was too far away to hear what was being said but he saw Dyer suddenly make a play for his gun. He wanted to shout out, to warn Jack.

But it would have been pointless. Jack's Peacemaker was already clear of its holster and levelled at Dyer. It boomed like thunder, the sound reverberating around the gravestones. Dyer screamed and toppled backwards, his gun spinning to the ground as he clutched his hand. The gunmetal heliographed the sunlight. Jack fired the Peacemaker a second time and Dyer spun around. He landed on his back near Avril Dyer's grave.

Brad broke from the trees and rushed

over to Jack. Dyer lay near his mother's grave, still screaming in pain.

Jack had turned away and started stalking back toward the trees. As he reached Brad, Brad said, 'Jack, he's still alive.'

Jack nodded and Brad noticed a tear rolling down the black man's cheek.

'I've stopped him,' Jack said. 'That's what I came here to do.'

Brad turned to Dyer. He writhed in the dirt in agony. Jack had shot both his hands. A bullet through each. They were covered in blood and hung uselessly from Dyer's wrists. Brad wheeled after Jack.

'You didn't kill him,' he said.

'I never said I would. I said I'd stop him. I've done that. He won't be able to hold a gun ever again. In *either* hand.'

'I thought we were going to kill him.'

'If you want to kill him,' Jack said pointing to Dyer, 'go and do it. I can't.'

218

Brad looked back at Dyer. He had no desire to kill him. Screaming at the top of his lungs, writhing in pain, he looked pitiful, pathetic. 'Jack,' Brad said, 'I don't understand. Why didn't you just kill him? He killed your brother.'

Jack stopped and faced Brad. He shook his head. 'No, Brad, no he didn't.' He looked at Dyer and another tear cascaded down his cheek. 'He *is* my brother, Brad.'

# 16

Jack felt devoid of emotion as he walked down Cedar Street followed by Brad. He had done what he had set out to do; no more, no less. He felt relief that he had stopped Dyer but also a profound sense of sympathy for all the people Dyer had hurt before he had managed to catch up with him.

'I don't understand,' Brad said. 'Your *brother*?'

Jack knew he owed Brad a full explanation. He would tell the tale one last time. He could forget it all then. Dyer had been stopped. He could return to Norma and continue living life as he had done before he had set out on this manhunt. 'Come on,' he told Brad. 'I'll buy you a drink.'

They walked on to the main drag and Jack stopped a young tousle-haired boy who was running and playing in the snow. He held up a dollar before the boy's wide gaze. 'Listen,' he said. 'I want you to go get the doctor and tell him there's a man in the cemetery who needs his help. Will you do that?'

The boy nodded, snatched the dollar and ran off shouting, 'Doc Perkins, come quick!'

Jack and Brad entered the Six Shot Saloon and Jack ordered whiskey for them both. The evening drinkers had started filling the place so they found a corner table and Jack began. 'Dyer's real name is Richard,' he said. 'Richard Hart. He's my older brother.'

Brad frowned. 'But . . .'

'I know what you're going to say,' Jack interrupted. 'He's white and I'm black. Well, I suppose you could say we're actually half-brothers. We had different mothers. But we were brought up as brothers and that's what we are. Our father, John Hart, always made sure that he treated us equally. He's a good man.'

'Is he the feller who works for the

US Marshals' office? The one who arranged your badge?'

Jack nodded. 'We agreed that I would come and stop Dyer the way I did. That's why he wanted me to do the job. He didn't want his son killed any more than I wanted my brother killed.'

Brad looked confused.

'I'll start at the beginning,' Jack said. 'John Hart was an Englishman who settled in Colorado. He built a small ranch there and, after a few years, met Avril Dyer. John fell in love with her and they got married. A year later, they had a son, Richard.

'John loved Richard the moment he was born, but Avril turned sour on the idea of bringing up kids. Seems she was only interested in one thing: money. She told John as much and when Richard was only six months old, she left the ranch to go back to Black River, where she had come from. She told John to tell their son that she was dead and when Richard was old enough, that's what he was told.'

'She left her husband and son?' Brad asked.

Jack nodded. 'My pa says she had fooled him when he had first met her. She only married him because he was becoming prosperous. When Richard was born, she didn't take to the job of mothering. So she packed her bags and went, calling herself Avril Dyer again.'

Brad nodded, taking it in.

'Eight months later,' Jack continued, 'my pa met Jean. She was a beautiful black woman who came to his ranch as a housekeeper. Soon, John had fallen in love with her. He didn't care about what folk would say, she being black, and he learned that she felt the same for him as he did for her. They couldn't get married because he was still married to Avril legally. But they lived together as man and wife and soon I was born.'

'So they brought you and Richard up as brothers?'

'Only my pa did,' Jack said sadly.

'My ma died just after I was born.'

Brad nodded and sipped his drink.

'He brought us up well,' Jack said. 'We used to be close, me and Richard. When I was nine and he was eleven, we started playing at being gunfighters. My pa had two old guns and we'd take them out to the meadow and draw against each other. The guns weren't loaded, of course. Pa kept the bullets in a box on top of his wardrobe and we weren't allowed to touch them. So we'd have mock gunfights with the unloaded guns.'

'Like you did at the cabin with Patrick,' Brad interrupted.

Jack nodded. 'I won every time. Richard was fast but somehow I could always beat him. It began to rankle him. Soon, he set out to beat me at everything we did.' He took a sip of his drink. 'But he never could.'

'That's how you knew you could beat him in a gunfight,' Brad said, nodding with understanding. 'And that's what you meant in Bull's Creek when you said you'd beaten him at least a hundred times before.' He thought for a moment. 'So that's why he shot up your hand? Because you always beat him?'

'No,' Jack said, as he took another sip of his drink. 'Even though he was sore at me, he would have never done anything like that.' He paused and his mind returned to the well-trodden ground of the past. 'Until he fell in the pond,' he said. 'We used to play at a pond on our land. We'd go jumping on the rocks in the water. One day, Richard tried to outdo me by jumping out on to a rock in the deep water. He fell in. I managed to save him but . . . ' He shrugged. 'He had almost drowned. His brain was damaged.'

'He went crazy?' Brad asked.

Jack shook his head. 'Not crazy, no. His mind twisted things around. He started having nightmares about drowning. That's understandable, I guess, but the day at the pond had a lasting effect on him. The rivalry he felt for me started to eat him up inside.

He wasn't playing any more. A couple of weeks later, he said he wanted us to have a gunfight in the meadow. One last time, he said, before we got too old to play at being gunfighters. We went off behind the house and I remember feeling happy to be out there on a sunny day playing with my older brother. But there was something I didn't know.' He drained his glass. 'Richard had loaded his gun. He had climbed up on to Pa's wardrobe and gotten a handful of bullets out of the box and pushed them into his gun.'

'He tried to kill you?'

Jack nodded sadly. 'We squared off in the meadow and drew our guns. I beat him, of course, but this time it didn't matter. I squeezed my trigger and the hammer clicked on an empty chamber. Richard drew his weapon and it seemed to explode. I felt searing pain in my hand, then numbness as I fell over and blacked out. Richard had meant to kill me. He thought he *had* killed me. He ran away.'

Brad downed his drink. He thought for a moment then said, 'But that still doesn't explain why he's calling himself John Dyer.'

Jack shrugged. 'He took on another identity. Before the accident at the pond, he was angry with himself because he couldn't beat me at anything. Once his mind started twisting everything around, he probably hated Richard Hart so much he started to believe he was someone else; John Dyer. He knew Dyer was his mother's maiden name and John is his father's first name. So he created John Dyer. And John Dyer was nothing like Richard Hart; John Dyer was an outlaw. Richard became Dyer and started killing.'

'And believed he had killed Richard Hart?'

'That's why he couldn't face me at the cemetery at first. His mind has twisted the events of the day he shot me. He's convinced himself he killed Richard Hart on that day. But I know the truth and, deep down, so does he.

When he faced me, he remembered what really happened. And when he remembers he's Richard Hart, he must feel an awful guilt. He tried to kill his own brother and he's been murdering and thieving ever since. That's why he's been trying to convince himself Richard is dead. That way, he can go on as Dyer and live out the fantasy his mind has created. It protects him from having to think about the bad things he's done.'

'But not any more,' Brad said.

'No, not any more,' Jack agreed. 'When my pa found out about a man calling himself John Dyer leaving a trail of killing, he knew it was Richard. He knew he had to be stopped but he didn't want to have his own son killed. He remembered my hand and we agreed that I would find Dyer and fix it so that he couldn't kill anyone else ever again.'

Brad looked around the saloon, seemingly lost in thought. Then he said,

'But why did he come here to kill his mother? You said he was brought up believing she was dead.'

'He was,' Jack confirmed. 'Somehow, he must have discovered she hadn't died all those years ago but had returned to Black River. But by the time he had found the truth, she really was dead. He wanted to kill her for one simple reason: she is Richard Hart's mother. And as far as Dyer is concerned, he wants to erase all trace of Richard Hart's existence. That's why he was so desperate to kill me. I'm sure that after Avril, he would have gone after our pa. He probably thought that if he killed everyone connected with Richard, he would kill Richard's memory. And that's really all he was running from: a memory.'

Jack looked into his empty glass, watching the light reflect off the amber pool of whiskey in the bottom. He felt tired.

'What now?' Brad asked.

'Now,' Jack said, 'we go home.'

'What about your brother?'

'He'll be looked after here until he recovers. After that, it's up to him. If he wants to come home, my pa will be waiting. If he wants to stay away, that's fine too. But he can't hurt anyone any more.'

'I suppose it's time for me to return to my own family,' Brad said. He pulled the Raven amulet from under his shirt and watched it spinning on the chain. 'I want to see Laura and my pa but I want to get back to Kate as well.'

'It's best to see your family first,' Jack said. 'If you don't, you'll always be wondering about them. Do it now before it's too late. Unfinished family business has a habit of catching up with you sooner or later.'

Brad smiled and nodded. 'Yeah, I guess you found that out. Well then, Jack, if you're heading back to Colorado, I'll ride with you as far as Little Springs, Wyoming.'

Jack nodded and they got up and

headed outside into the evening sunlight. A light coat of snow had covered the town.

'We'd best get a pair of good horses,' Brad suggested. 'We've got a hard ride ahead of us.'

'Yeah,' Jack agreed. 'But not as hard as the ride here.'

# 17

As he approached the house where he had grown up, Brad felt his throat tighten. He was shaking. He was glad Jack was waiting for him in town; he didn't want his friend to see him like this. The house was as he remembered it. Its familiar look scared him. He had run away from this house and the man who lived in it.

Being here again brought back memories; good and bad memories. He remembered playing in the fields with his sister; he remembered trying to please his father, trying to wrench some words of praise from his mouth but receiving instead a string of curses; he remembered his mother and Laura giving him the Raven amulet the day he went off to war. The day he ran away.

He dismounted and hitched his horse

to the rail in front of the house. Swallowing hard, he stepped on to the porch and wiped his hands on his pants before knocking softly on the door.

A sound came from within, the creak of a chair followed by the shuffling sound of someone approaching. The door swung open slightly and a face appeared in the opening.

Brad recognized his father immediately. He looked older but his features were unmistakable. He squinted at Brad through his spectacles. 'Oh, it's you. I guess you'd better come in.' He turned away from the door and shuffled back down the hallway to the living-room.

Brad hesitated, unsure of his next move. His father had shown no emotion at seeing him after all these years. Brad looked at his horse. He could leave now, just go. But he remembered Jack's words of advice: if he didn't see his family now, he would always be wondering what might have happened if he had. He stepped into the house and followed his pa into the living-room.

The old man sat down in a chair near the fireplace and rubbed his knees. 'Goddamn joints,' he muttered.

Brad looked around the room. Now that his mother was dead, it lacked a woman's touch. The furniture had been arranged haphazardly. He noticed a photograph on the mantelpiece, taken at the same time as the photograph he had been studying in his office in Bull's Creek.

'That's my family,' his father said. He pointed to the faces in the picture. 'That's Edna, my wife. She's dead now, God rest her soul. That's Laura, my daughter. She's married to a banker in town. He's all right, I guess, but he knows nothing about cattle so we don't talk much 'cos I know nothing about banking.' He pointed at Brad's young, smiling face in the picture. 'That there's my son Brad. He went off and got himself killed in the war.' He paused. 'At least he must have got killed 'cos he never came home afterward. He was a good boy. He would have come home to help me with the ranch if he hadn't been killed. Always good with his hands, that boy.'

Brad stood looking at the picture dumbly, stunned. His father didn't recognize him! He thought he had been killed all those years ago. But even more shocking was hearing his pa calling him a good boy. *A good boy*. His father's own words.

'I suppose you'll want to see the fence,' his pa said.

'Fence?' He felt detached, confused.

'You came to fix the fence, didn't ya? That's my daughter, always interfering. I tell her last week that the fence is broke and she sends someone round to fix it. I don't need her sending no goddamn handymen round; I can look after myself.' He rose from the chair and led Brad to the kitchen. Pointing out the window, he said, 'Out back. There's tools and lumber in the barn.' He shuffled off again and Brad heard the chair creak as he sat back down in the other room.

Brad felt hot, stinging tears slide down his face. He wondered how much of a shock it would be to his pa if he told him he was his son. He considered doing just that, but stopped himself. *He thinks I was killed in the war. He can live with that. I can't go in there and tell him what a bad father he was. Let him live with his memories of the son who was killed, the boy who would have returned if he could have. I can't tell him I ran away because of him.*

He went out into the cool wind and felt it drying his tears. All this time he had thought his father was disappointed with him, he had been wrong. *A good boy.* His pa remembered him as a good son. Those were the only words of praise he had ever heard from his father and he had had to come here so many years after running away to hear them. Hearing them had a dual effect on him; he felt happy, as if a weight had been lifted from him, but he also felt immeasurably sad because all these years he had been running from a memory of his father which was false, nothing more than an illusion.

Why didn't he tell me *then*, offer some words of encouragement? Things would have turned out so differently.

He stood in the cold breeze for a while, thinking of the father he had run away from and the old man sitting in the house, believing his son was dead.

He went to the barn, found the tools and lumber and started to fix the fence.

★ ★ ★

By the time he got back to the house, his pa was waiting in the kitchen. The old man studied Brad closely from behind his glasses. 'When you see my daughter again,' he said, 'you tell her I said I don't need no more handymen coming round and that I can take care of myself.' He paused then added, 'But you can tell her you noticed the barn needs a lick of paint. Don't tell her I said so, just that you noticed it when you was fetching the tools.'

Brad nodded and his pa held out his frail hand. Brad shook it. 'Could you tell me where I might find your daughter, Mr Harris? I need to see about being paid for fixing your fence.'

'Well, today's Sunday so she'll be at the cemetery putting flowers on the graves. Does it every Sunday, she does, without fail.'

'Graves?' Brad asked.

'Edna's and Brad's.'

*Brad's?* Brad felt a coldness run through him. All the years he had been drifting around the country, there was a grave here with his name on it.

His pa led him to the front door and opened it. Brad stepped past him and unhitched his horse. As he swung into the saddle, the old man said, 'Of course Brad's grave isn't really a grave. No body in it. They never found his body.'

Brad said nothing. He wheeled the horse around and tipped his hat to his father.

'Mister?' his pa said from the porch.

Brad turned around in the saddle and looked at the old man. Standing there on the porch, shivering against the cold, he looked so old, so vulnerable. 'When Brad was a boy, I wasn't a good father to him. I used to curse him lots, the way my father cursed me. I guess I didn't know no other way. You know, I wouldn't blame him if he just didn't bother coming back after the war was done. Just went off and found himself a wife and lived somewhere far away from here.'

Brad felt his throat tighten. Did his pa know who he was? Had he realized?

'You live near here?' his father asked.

Brad shook his head. 'Idaho.'

'That's pretty far,' the old man said softly, nodding. 'Pretty far.'

'It isn't that far,' Brad offered.

'You got a wife?'

Brad thought of Kate. 'I'm working on it.'

The old man nodded again and said,

'Well if you and your wife are ever by this way and need a place to stay, I got plenty of room. Be sure to come and visit.'

Brad nodded and felt his eyes fill with tears. 'I will,' he said weakly. He spurred his horse on and rode away from the house, looking back only once.

And when he did look back, his pa was still on the porch, his frail body shaking as he wept.

★ ★ ★

Brad got to the small, hilltop cemetery before Laura. The flowers on the graves were dead and withered; she hadn't replaced them yet. When he saw his mother's gravestone, he wept and remembered the woman who had brought him up. The most vivid memory he had of his mother was when she and Laura had given him the Raven talisman.

When he looked at his own grave,

240

marked by a cold stone cross, a shiver ran up his spine. At first, it frightened him to think that this grave with his name on it had stood in this cemetery since the war ended. But then he realized how much he had changed since going to war. He had become independent, strong. Perhaps the Brad Harris everyone in Little Springs, Wyoming, remembered really was dead.

He decided then that he would not wait for Laura to arrive. He was going to come back. And he was going to bring Kate and Patrick back with him. He could meet Laura and her banker husband then, make it a proper reunion.

Still, he felt guilty about going home without leaving some sign for Laura that he had been here, that he was alive.

He looked at his own gravestone then smiled as an idea came to him.

# 18

Brad found Jack waiting for him in the saloon. 'How did it go?' the black man asked.

Brad smiled. 'All right. I saw my father. I fixed his fence for him.' He laughed, then let out a sigh. He was sure it was a sigh of relief. 'He was nothing like the tyrant I remembered, Jack. He's changed a hell of a lot.'

'Maybe,' Jack replied. 'Or maybe you have.'

Brad shrugged.

'Did you see your sister?'

'No,' Brad said. 'I've decided I'm going to come back, bring Kate and Patrick. I want to do this properly, Jack. A real reunion.'

Jack smiled. 'Speaking of reunions, I was thinking of bringing Norma out west, maybe visit you and Kate. After all, I want to get my stallion back.'

Brad laughed. 'Don't worry, we'll take good care of him in the meantime.'

They left the saloon and unhitched their horses from the rail. As they swung into their saddles, Jack said, 'It's been good riding with you, Brad.'

They shook hands and Brad said, 'Same here, Jack. Give my best to Norma.'

'I will,' Jack said, 'I will. You know, I've been thinking some while I've been waiting for you here. Maybe it's time me and Norma started another family of our own. We can't go running from the past forever.'

'Well, I wish you luck,' Brad said. He spurred his horse on and headed down the main drag, eager to return to Kate.

'Hey, Brad,' Jack shouted after him.

Brad stopped and turned back to his friend.

'Your sister's going to be angry when she finds out you went to see your father but didn't see her too.'

'It's all right,' he shouted back. 'I

left her a message.' He spurred the horse on again, heading for the distant mountains where all traces of the earlier storms had vanished.

Perhaps winter wouldn't be so bad this year after all.

# Epilogue

Laura walked along the path to her mother's and brother's graves, her arms full of vividly-coloured, sweet-smelling flowers. She came here every Sunday and put flowers on the graves, replacing the dead ones from the week before. Coming here was a ritual she performed every week because she had loved her mother and brother when they had been alive.

Today, though, something was different. As she approached the graves, Laura noticed something that took her breath away. She squinted against the sunlight to be sure of what she had seen. When she was sure, she put her hands to her mouth in shock and ran to the graves, leaving a bright trail of tumbling flowers behind her.

By the time she reached the graves,

she was crying, only half believing what she was seeing.

On Brad's gravestone, hanging from the cross, glinting sharply in the sunlight, was the Raven.

Laura picked up the silver talisman and held it tightly. She felt the wind drying her tears and she smiled. She had always suspected Brad was still alive. Now she knew. He had been here and he had left her this sign. He would be coming back.

Laura picked up the scattered, fragile flowers from the ground and placed them on her mother's grave before running back down the hill toward her father's house.

She knew he would be glad to see the Raven. Brad was coming home after all these years.

As she left the cemetery, a light flurry of snow tumbled to the earth, turning everything white, pristine and new.

## THE CROOKED SHERIFF
**John Dyson**

Black Pete Bowen quit Texas with a burning hatred of men who try to take the law into their own hands. But he discovers that things aren't much different in the silver mountains of Arizona.

## THEY'LL HANG BILLY FOR SURE:
**Larry & Stretch**
**Marshall Grover**

Billy Reese, the West's most notorious desperado, was to stand trial. From all compass points came the curious and the greedy, the riff-raff of the frontier. Suddenly, a crazed killer was on the loose — but the Texas Trouble-Shooters were there, girding their loins for action.

## RIDERS OF RIFLE RANGE
### Wade Hamilton

Veterinarian Jeff Jones did not like open warfare — but it was there on Scrub Pine grass. When he diagnosed a sick bull on the Endicott ranch as having the contagious blackleg disease, he got involved in the warfare — whether he liked it or not!


## BEAR PAW
### Nevada Carter

Austin Dailey traded two cows to a pair of Indians for a bay horse, which subsequently disappeared. Tracks led to a secret hideout of fugitive Indians — and cattle thieves. Indians and stockmen co-operated against the rustlers. But it was Pale Woman who acted as interpreter between her people and the rangemen.